THE
HOUSE
ON
CHARLTON
STREET

Dola de Jong

THE
HOUSE
ON
CHARLTON
STREET

Illustrated by **Gilbert Riswold**

CHARLES SCRIBNER'S SONS   NEW YORK

For Ian

Contents

THE
HOUSE
ON
CHARLTON
STREET

CHAPTER ONE

What's So Good
about Old?

The five Bartletts were at supper, squeezed around the table in the small dining room of their Greenwich Village apartment in New York. It was a cold supper of tunafish salad, cucumbers in sour cream, brown bread, and iced tea—all things that didn't involve pots and pans. Mrs. Bartlett just hadn't felt like cooking, because her stove would heat up the tiny kitchen even more. It was a real Indian summer—hot and humid. New York was steaming all over again. It seemed as if all the brick and glass of the big city still contained the summer heat, as if the cold spell earlier in September had never happened.

Mr. Bartlett, whose first name was Carl, hadn't suffered from the high temperature at all, since his law offices uptown were air-conditioned. His mood and appetite were as good as ever. Next to him sat Mrs. Jessica Bartlett, who looked very cheerful in a bright yellow smock. She was trying hard to feel equally cheerful after a long, hot day in her weaving studio, around the corner.

John Bartlett, sixteen, and already just about as tall as his father, who measured six feet, sat on her other side. John looked serious because he had started his senior year in high school this fall. Tonight he was wondering how many hours his homework would take.

Slumped in her chair next to John was Phoebe Bartlett, who would be fourteen in another week. She was most uncomfortable in a wool sweater, which she was wearing because, as she had just finished saying, "*Nobody* wears summer clothes after Labor Day."

David Bartlett, eleven years old, completed the circle around the table. He, too, was quite tall for his age. In addition he was muscular, because even though he was a quiet sort of boy, he was a good athlete. Right this minute David was shoveling big forkfuls of tunafish into his mouth and was much concerned with the prospects of seconds.

The Bartletts had, in addition, three boarders: the tomcat, who for some reason had been named Porto Rico, and who these days actually resided in the next-door yard near a pure Siamese lady friend, who wasn't allowed out of her house. And there were Phoebe's birds, Parakeet-He and Parakeet-She, to be precise, who lived in a cage in her room.

All the tall windows in the old-fashioned apartment were

wide open, and as none of the Bartletts had known what to say after Phoebe's pronouncement on fall fashions, the big-city sounds from outside seemed extra loud. There were the noises of a bus starting up with a puff and a screech, shrill voices of children roller skating on the sidewalk, and the rhythmic scraping of their skates on the pavement. In the middle of the street some big boys were playing baseball with the usual amount of cheering and arguing. Two women were in busy conversation on the stoop downstairs, their voices droning on and on. And high in the sky sounded the different droning of a plane in the process of climbing away from the city into the clouds.

Then, on top of all that, "the lady downstairs" started to play the piano.

"There we go again. . . ." John said in a resigned tone of voice, without interrupting his meal for a second.

But Mrs. Bartlett put down her fork and turned to Mr. Bartlett. "I think I would like to go to a movie tonight," she said with a big sigh.

"How about us?" Phoebe pointed her fork at the two boys and then at herself. "You just came back from the studio," she reminded Mrs. Bartlett, "but I, for one—little unimportant I—have been home since three-fifteen. She was playing the same piece then, and on and on till five o'clock . . ." Phoebe interrupted herself, and turning to her father she fairly yelled, "Can't you *do* something about it, Daddy?"

"Don't point with your fork," was all Mr. Bartlett remarked.

"Nobody can," John answered her, in the same dry tone of voice he had used before.

"Let's bore a hole through the floor and pour some . . . some paint into her piano," David suggested helpfully. He had thought about it last night in bed and in the foggy mood right before sleep it had seemed an excellent idea. Now it didn't, and he felt a little self-conscious when the family ignored his suggestion as just too silly to consider.

Mrs. Evelyn Hough, "the lady downstairs," as they called her, was their landlady. She owned the dilapidated brownstone building and made her home on the first floor. Recently she had acquired a piano, and now she pounded away for hours on end. But, in John's words, she should have provided the Bartletts with five sets of earplugs, because she knew exactly three piano pieces, which she played over and over again at all hours of the day and night. Old brownstone buildings like hers had originally been built for single families, not for apartment living. Every sound carried through the floors.

The one bothered most by the landlady's musical endeavor was John, who was something of a musical prodigy and had set his mark on becoming a professional musician. He attended the famous New York High School of Music and Art and studied the oboe. Because of her consideration for the neighbors, Mrs. Bartlett had a small part of her weaving studio on Eleventh Street partitioned off for him. There, in a small corner of the big loft where Mrs. Bartlett, a hand weaver by profession, wove her large carpets and wall hangings, John could practice to his heart's content. So the constant keyboard pounding of Mrs. Hough didn't disturb him at his practice, yet when he was home he felt that the sounds emanating from downstairs were slowly but surely killing every desire to devote his life to music. When he said that, he was joking of course, but the playing bothered him even more than it did the others.

Phoebe had put the question to her parents whether "the lady downstairs" did not realize that her constant practicing would be annoying to her upstairs neighbors and tenants, the Bartletts. And Mr. Bartlett had said a thing or two about consideration for others, which he found was sorely missing nowadays.

"Let's write her a letter and slip it under her door," Phoebe now suggested.

"Let's not," Mr. Bartlett said. Then, after exchanging a look and a nod with his wife, he went on. "We wanted to tell you anyway—we're going to move. We've bought a house!"

"When? . . . Where? . . ." Phoebe shouted.

"You're kidding," John said.

But David was silent. He felt a funny twinge somewhere near his stomach. Suddenly the tunafish salad left much to be desired.

David had lived in this apartment all his life. Even though the other members of his family complained about "the lady downstairs," who in every respect was utterly indifferent to the comfort and rights of her tenants, David was happy in the apartment.

In his tiny room he had enough space to put his toys away. His Dad, a first-class carpenter, had provided him with shelves all around the wall. His clothes were in a couple of cardboard boxes under his bed, not because he had no chest of drawers, but simply that he needed that piece of furniture for more important things: his collections, in fact. He just couldn't understand why his mother objected to that arrangement, but at last he had won that argument.

As to the rest of the apartment, what was so bad about it, David wondered. The hall was long and narrow. When he was younger, it had always been excellent for roller skating, for an ambush at cowboy games, for parades of toy soldiers, and for kick ball—that is, when Mrs. Bartlett was out.

The piano playing of "the lady downstairs" was all right with him. It put him to sleep at night. David regarded listening to her repetitious playing as something similar to counting sheep. He watched for her mistakes and kept score. When she hit a wrong note, it was a point for him. If, by chance, she got it right, it was a point for her. Her playing was the best of sleeping pills—surely a whole lot better than the ones advertised on television. David would listen, keep score, and the next thing he knew would be the ringing of his alarm

clock in the morning. The idea of pouring paint through a hole in the floor had occurred to him only because he had tried to accommodate his family.

No, as far as David was concerned, they could stay in this apartment until he was ready to depart for college—another seven years away. However, Mother and Dad had bought a house and there certainly was nothing he could do about it. They were now answering John's and Phoebe's eager questions. So David decided to pay some attention.

"You know that street below Houston Street," Dad was saying. "Charlton Street. I'm sure you've been through it. It's on the other side of Sixth Avenue, the west side. One of these days we'll go to the New York Historical Society and do some research on the history of Charlton Street. And Grandma could tell us stories about it. Grandpa was born there. His parents lived on that street until they died. It's a very old street."

"What's so good about *old?*" David mumbled to himself, but loud enough to be understood by John, who had extraordinarily fine hearing.

"What's wrong with *old*, Boxhead?" John asked.

"Everything," David said angrily. "I like modern, like those new apartment houses they put up everywhere around here. If you wanted to move so badly from an old apartment," he continued, looking at his father, "why didn't you rent one of those modern apartments in the new buildings? That would have been great."

Before Mr. Bartlett could answer him, Phoebe gave a loud exaggerated sigh and rolled her eyes toward the ceiling. "That child has no feeling for tradition," she exclaimed in despair.

"Child, yourself," David came back. He had no idea what she meant by "tradition," but he wouldn't let her get away with calling him "child."

"Phoebe, would you clear the table and bring the dessert?" Mother asked.

"What's for dessert?" David wanted to know.

"Ice cream," Mother told him. Then she said, "Aren't you interested in the new house, David? I think you didn't even listen when Dad told about it."

David shrugged his shoulders. "Not much," he said.

Phoebe, busily collecting the dirty plates, was about to lecture him again, but Mr. Bartlett cut her off with, "All right, Phoebe. . . ." To David he said, "After dinner you and I will take a stroll over to Charlton Street and have a good look. The house needs a lot done to it before we'll move in. Did you finish your homework?"

"Yes. But I can't go with you. Len is coming over. We're going to play ball in the park."

"Then Len can come with us," Mr. Bartlett decided. "There'll be time to play ball afterwards. I'll join you for a game. I feel like getting some exercise before I take Mother to the movies."

When Mr. Bartlett talked in that tone of voice, very quiet

and clipped, David knew that he wouldn't stand for an argument. All right, he thought, they would stare at the crummy house and have one of those tame games afterwards. No rough stuff, no fights when Dad was along.

Just the same, he had to admit that Dad wasn't a bad catcher for his age. To be honest, Dad was a better catcher than David—better even, than Len, David's best friend, who was tops in athletics. Len liked to play ball with David's father. His own father never came out to Washington Square Park to play with Len, and Len had told David that he envied him for having a father like that.

While David waited for his ice cream to get softer, helping it along with his spoon, he thought that it would be kind of nice to have Len see the house on Charlton Street. Would Len ever be surprised! Maybe they could have fun in that old house. Maybe there were secret doors and underground passages. He felt himself getting excited. He looked up at his father. "Gee, Dad, when did you buy it? And what does it look like inside? And where did you get the money?" he asked.

Again Phoebe rolled up her eyes. "He kills me," she sighed. But Mr. and Mrs. Bartlett and John smiled.

"That's what's called a delayed reaction," John said. "Hey, Boxhead," he added goodnaturedly, "did you hear the news? Mother and Dad have bought a house and we're going to move."

"What's this 'Boxhead'?" Mother inquired. "It sounds awful."

"A name of endearment," John explained. He pushed his chair back from the table and reached out to rumple David's hair. "He's my favorite brother," he kidded. "May I be excused?" he then asked. "I've got about forty hours of homework tonight."

"Big shot!" David said, although he didn't mind anything John did or said. He knew John was fond of him. He wasn't so sure about Phoebe. So John could call him anything he liked, whereas Phoebe had better just call him by his rightful name.

"Oh, look at your hair now," Phoebe giggled.

Quickly David smoothed it down with his hands, but it was too late.

"Haircut tomorrow, David," Mother told him.

"Yes, ma'am," David said.

While Phoebe washed the dishes and Mr. and Mrs. Bartlett were reading the evening papers in the living room, David leaned out of the window, watching for Leonard Harvey Chase—Len, for short—to come around the corner. David couldn't wait to tell him the big news. . . .

CHAPTER TWO

Moving Day

It was Saturday, the fifteenth of October—moving day for the Bartletts.

"The misery of it all," Phoebe sighed, while she dragged two shopping bags full of odds and ends through the narrow hall. The hall itself was already full of odds and ends. Phoebe was having a hard time, navigating between an upended mattress against one wall and piled-up cartons against the other. Things kept slipping out of her shopping bags—a comb, a ragged toy kitten, a tangle of belts and a bunch of picture post cards.

David, in the spirit of moving day, picked up behind her. However, he couldn't help but say, "Some packing you did!"

"Thank you kindly," Phoebe said haughtily and stumbled

out of the apartment, down the stairs, and on her way to Charlton Street.

She didn't even look behind her, David thought. She just left like that, even though she has lived here for eleven years. When John and Dad had left, they each had made a little speech. "Well, here goes," John had said. He had given the living room door a slap in passing, as if to say goodbye.

Dad had looked into every empty room with a funny expression on his face. "Leaving a lot of memories," he had said to John, and then he had gone back to the kitchen, where Mother was, and come out looking very thoughtful. Then Dad and John had picked up their precious cargo—a hamper with John's oboe and recorder, some antique china, a piece of sculpture, several paintings, and Phoebe's birds in their cage—and were gone.

The movers had carried most of the furniture down and were now loading the van in front of the building. Mrs. Bartlett was in the kitchen packing the breakfast dishes and making conversation with a dejected Porto Rico in his carrier. David wandered back to the kitchen.

Mrs. Bartlett gave him a searching look. "Do you feel funny about moving?" she asked kindly.

David just nodded.

"I know exactly how you feel," his mother went on. "I feel funny myself, and so did Dad. Somehow I'll miss this apartment, though I won't miss that. . . ." She pointed her index finger down front, from where piano music came floating up. It sounded loud and hollow in the empty apartment.

"The lady downstairs," no doubt awakened at seven by the arrival of the movers and prevented from going back to sleep by the racket, had decided on a farewell concert. Now, at nine o'clock, in a valiant struggle to drown out the noises outside her door, or maybe in a last-ditch stand against her departing tenants, she was still pounding away at one of the three pieces in her repertoire.

The boss of the movers, a huge man with freckles, graying hair, and a jolly disposition, stuck his head around the kitchen door. "Anything else to go here?" he asked.

"I just have to tie up this carton," Mrs. Bartlett told him. "It'll take me a minute."

"Take your time," he answered. "Take your time, Mrs. Bartlett. Mind if I have a drink of chlorinated?" He went up to the sink and drew a glass of water. While he drank it down he rested his big frame against the sink. Then he took a large handkerchief out of his pants pocket and gave his perspiring face and neck a good going over.

David watched him with admiration. Mr. O'Connor was able to carry large pieces of furniture down the narrow stairs, all by himself, as if he were a young man. David would have liked to talk to him, but he didn't know how to start.

"I'm sorry it's such an impossible staircase, Mr. O'Connor," Mrs. Bartlett said.

"Don't worry about it," Mr. O'Connor said cheerfully.

"We're used to it. We'll have more trouble in Charlton Street. The doors in that building are like a needle's eye."

Mrs. Bartlett gave him a surprised look. "How do you know?" she asked.

"That house used to be like home to me," Mr. O'Connor said. "I haven't been inside the place for about forty years. But I know it like the nose on my face. Boy, the stories that house could tell!"

"Did you live there?" David asked, not quite sure about the question.

Mr. O'Connor started to smile, as if he were remembering something pleasant. "I didn't precisely live there," he told David, "but I darned near did. My mother used to work in that house some fifty years ago, when I was a little feller. She used to bake cookies for me in that big kitchen, and after school I used to go over to stuff my face. They were good cookies, I remember. They don't bake them that way nowadays."

"Oh, imagine that!" Mrs. Bartlett exclaimed. "Tell me, what was the house like then? Who lived there? Isn't it exciting, David, to think that Mr. O'Connor knew the house so long ago?"

"Yeah," David said. He tried to picture Mr. O'Connor as a small boy, but he just couldn't.

"They were strange people," Mr. O'Connor said, still reminiscing. "The couple my mother worked for, that is . . . Their name was MacLaughlin, if I remember correctly." He shook his head and touched his hand to his brow to indicate how strange the old couple had been. "My mother never talked about them in those early days, but after they died she did. You know, things happened there that people still don't understand." He shook his head again. Then he put his handkerchief back in his pocket and started to walk away from the sink toward the door. "I'm standing here gabbing," he said. "I'd better get a move on."

"I've *got* to hear these stories," Mrs. Bartlett said determinedly. "Please, Mr. O'Connor, won't you come to see us some evening? Some time when you're not too busy, maybe?"

"Oho . . ." Mr. O'Connor laughed. "I see I started something. I'll tell you what, Mrs. Bartlett: when I move you out of your studio on Monday, and after we get those big looms of yours safely up to the fourth floor in your new house, you'll make me a nice strong cup of coffee and I'll give you the low-down on the MacLaughlins. Right?"

"Oh, how nice of you, Mr. O'Connor," Mrs. Bartlett exclaimed. "I can't wait. . . ."

"You bet," Mr. O'Connor assured her. "It'll break the monotony for me."

When he had left the kitchen, Mrs. Bartlett turned to David. "See, darling," she said, "that's what's so wonderful about an old house. An old house is like an adventure—an adventure into the past. . . ." David was thinking how young his mother looked. Not like a mother, but like a girl—and especially so today, because she wore jeans and an old shirt of Dad's, frayed at the collar and with the sleeves rolled up. And her face had smudges of dirt on it.

"Come on, dear," she now said. "Let's hurry. I've got to finish here and get over to Charlton Street. And poor Porto Rico . . . I don't want to leave him in the carrier longer than is necessary."

"He must be asleep, he's so quiet." David went over to the carrier on the floor in a corner, from which, indeed, there wasn't a sound. But when he knelt down to take a peek inside through the little window, he looked straight into Porto Rico's frightened eyes.

"Don't worry," David told the big tomcat, "you'll like the new house. Lots of fun and adventures there." Then he turned around to his mother. "Right, Ma?"

"Right, Son," she smiled. "See if you can find me a piece of string for this carton."

"Here you are. . . ." David pulled an end of cord out of one of his bulging pants pockets. Together they tied up the box.

"Can I go to the park now?" David asked. "Len and the other guys are meeting there at nine-thirty for a game."

Mrs. Bartlett gave him a searching look. She was obviously thinking it over. David felt himself getting red in the face. He knew he should stick around today, but he felt he wanted to get away from it all. Being with his friends in the park would, for a couple of hours at least, make it like any ordinary Saturday. After that he would just go to their new house and not feel so strange about it.

But his mother had made a different decision. He saw it in her face even before she told him. "Not today, David. We'll be needing you. I want to get the beds set up and made, and the kitchen in some order for Sunday morning breakfast. The sooner we get straightened out, the better. Monday I'm moving the studio. That takes a lot of supervising, with the different parts of the looms and the yarns. I need you today, David. You're a member of the family. You have responsibilities too, Son."

"Okay." All at once David felt better. His mother was probably right. He might have felt funny in the park, playing baseball, while the others were working so hard.

For a moment his mother put a hand on David's hands, which were busy tying a knot in the cord. "I'm glad you're here with me," she said gently. "We can leave the apartment together."

"Yeah." David couldn't say much more because he suddenly had trouble swallowing. He picked up the carton and carried it out of the kitchen, through the hall, and right on down the stairs. It was a heavy load, difficult to get down the staircase, but he managed. He put it down with a pile of other things on the sidewalk and went right on up for one of the cartons stacked in the hall. He kept at it, running up the stairs and going down with the heavy boxes, till he had moved every one of them.

He was wet all over with perspiration, his arms ached, and on the last trip down his legs were trembling in a funny way. But he felt great, and very much part of things.

Mr. O'Connor was standing in the van, storing away the last of the Bartletts' household belongings, which the other men were handing him. Now he climbed down into the street and came over to where David stood. "Make a muscle," he told David. And when David did, he tested it with his great thumb. "You're all right," he said. "I bet you're a good ball player. How about a ride over?" he asked.

"I'll ask my mother," David told him. He ran into the house and called his mother from the bottom of the stairs. When she appeared on the landing he shouted up to her, "Can I ride over on the truck? Mr. O'Connor asked me."

"Sure," she said. "I'm leaving too." Then she added, "I'll beat you to the house. Want to bet?"

"You couldn't! I'll bet you a pack of gum. . . ."

"You'll lose," she warned him. "You'll have to drive all the way around. I can walk straight over."

"Oh, yeah? . . ."

David ran back to the van. He climbed into the open back where Mr. O'Connor and one of his helpers were already standing, ready for departure. Up front in the cab the driver started the engine with a roar. The last thing David saw while driving off was his mother, coming down the front steps of the building with Porto Rico in his carrier. To David's astonishment she blew a gay kiss at "the lady downstairs," who had come to the window to watch the van leave.

The van was shaking something awful, but David, with his feet firmly planted and his arms akimbo, kept his balance. He secretly wished they would drive past the park where he knew Len and his other friends would be. He then would call out to them and they would see him, standing in the back of the truck.

And sure enough, the driver turned south on Fifth Avenue and swung right at the Washington Square Arch, where the boys usually played ball. David leaned out of the van, holding on to the side, and yelled Len's name as loudly as he could. Since there wasn't much traffic on Saturday mornings, Len heard him. Within seconds he had passed the word to the other boys, and all five of them started running after the large vehicle, catching up with it in no time at all. They sure were fast runners! Mr. O'Connor seemed to enjoy the pursuit, and when the van had to stop at a red light, he told the boys to climb on. He even gave them a helping hand.

"This is great," Len shouted, punching David on the arm.

The van proceeded west on Waverly Place, swung around into Sixth Avenue, and kept going, shaking and rattling along the bumpy thoroughfare. It was only a short ride to Charlton Street. Too short for the boys. But once in the street, it took a lot of maneuvering to get the huge truck turned and parked in front of Number 33½.

Mr. O'Connor let his big hulk down cautiously, and so

did the other movers, but the boys took the big jump down, one after the other. Then they assembled in front of the four-story, red-brick house with the green shutters and looked it over. They didn't say anything, but David could see from their expressions that they were impressed. Len had seen it, of course—several times, when he and David had gone there after school to see how the work on it was progressing. But he seemed to admire it all over again.

At that moment David felt really proud. For the first time he fully realized that this building, dating back to the beginning of the nineteenth century, was very special. It was as his father had said to him and Len on that night in September, when they first went to look at it. "This is a piece of American history, boys. In this country, especially in New York City nowadays, we're tearing down our landmarks." And Dad had looked kind of grim when he added, "And so help me, I'll see to it that this one will stay here for at least another fifty years."

The question, whether they could see the inside too, from one of the boys, brought David back to the present. The four movers had started to unload. David's father was helping Mr. O'Connor with the front door, which had to be taken off its hinges. His mother arrived, out of breath, and said to David in mock anger, "I'll get you your gum tomorrow," and then disappeared into the house. So David realized that this would be the wrong time for a guided tour. And he told the boys.

After they left, David walked slowly up the five worn steps of the stoop, past his father, past Mr. O'Connor, and into the marble front hall. He felt very special and very solemn.

CHAPTER THREE

Mrs. Bartlett Needs
a Shower

That next Monday when David came home from school he found his mother seated amidst boxes and barrels at the kitchen table. She didn't seem to mind the confusion in the kitchen and was busily writing in a notebook. In front of her on the table, next to the notebook, were two empty coffee cups, two cake plates with only some crumbs on them, and a cake platter with just one piece of raisin cake left.

"Hi," David said. "Can I have that piece of cake and what are you writing?"

"Hi . . . shhhh . . . yes, you may . . . just a minute," Mrs. Bartlett mumbled, writing furiously.

David removed a carton from a chair opposite her and sat down. He decided that the last piece of cake was too small

35

for sharing. Phoebe wasn't home from school yet. What she didn't know wouldn't bother her.

While he chewed his cake he watched his mother's pencil move swiftly over the page. Because he couldn't read her script upside down, her skill seemed miraculous, the writing even more mysterious. "What are you writing?" he asked again.

"Wait a minute," she urged him. "Don't talk!"

David looked around the large basement kitchen. He was going to like it more than any other part of the house. First of all, you could reach it directly from the street. You went through the gate, next to the stoop, down a few steps, then through a tall, iron-grated door, and at a left angle, you went through the entrance door to the kitchen. Just as it used to be in the olden days.

The Bartletts had decided to restore the kitchen to its original dignity. Before they bought the house it had been a small basement apartment. Now it was a large space in which many of the antiques which the Bartletts had gathered together through the years would be displayed. However, the pewter dishes and copper pots hadn't been unpacked yet because first the entire kitchen floor was going to be turned over.

It sounded funny, but actually it was quite a simple idea of Mr. Bartlett's. The floorboards were worn. In addition, people had covered them with so many coats of paint that it would be impossible to restore them. On Sunday morning David had found his father and John on their knees, carefully prying up one of the floorboards. They had managed, and found that the underside, though extremely dirty, was in

perfect condition. "Can you imagine!" Mr. Bartlett had exclaimed, quite excited. "Can you imagine . . . after all these many years, this wood has been preserved."

David had just stood there, not quite understanding what his father meant, but John had called Mrs. Bartlett and Phoebe in to let them share in the discovery. And then, when David heard the whole family discuss the quality and the width of the wood, and their praise of the workmanship of those olden days, he had joined in the excitement. And at this moment again he imagined the large trees which had been sawed by hand into these strong, wide boards.

"So . . ." Mrs. Bartlett said, interrupting his thoughts. "All done!" She leaned back in her chair with an expression of contentment. "Hi, feller," she then said, as if seeing David for the first time since he had come home from school.

"Hi, yourself," David said. "What were you scribbling?"

"Mr. O'Connor was here. He told me all he remembered about this house. I wrote it all down. I wanted to be sure that I wouldn't forget a thing." She stuck her hands into the pockets of her slacks and looked down on the notebook. "It's quite a story," she said, nodding her head and reflecting back on what she had heard.

"Tell me," David asked eagerly.

"At dinner . . . I'll recite the whole story so you can all hear." She looked at her watch. "Heavens, the pot roast!" she sighed, and got up to start preparations for supper.

"Can't you just tell me a little bit?" David asked.

Mrs. Bartlett took the meat out of the refrigerator. Then she looked around at him with a smile. "David," she said, "after all these eleven years of your existence you still amaze me." But there was so much affection in her voice that David wasn't worried about the fact that he puzzled his mother.

"Oh Ma," he pleaded, "don't be funny. Tell me just the bare facts. I'll wait for the rest."

She poured some oil into a pot and turned on the gas. After the soft plop of the burner she sang: "Hear ye, hear ye . . . David Bartlett. This house has a mystery. . . ." She added, "Those are the bare facts."

"Oh, gee," David said. He looked around the large room, where it was getting dark already, with a mixture of apprehension and excitement. He would have liked to ask more questions, but he knew that his mother would get annoyed with his insistence.

"How much homework do you have?" she asked.

"Not much," David said hopefully. Maybe she would let him sit in the kitchen with her for a while, and who knows, he still might be able to pry more out of her.

"In that case," she said, "you can help me unpack these boxes. You start while I get the pot roast going."

"Do I have to?" David asked.

"Yes, you do," Mrs. Bartlett said, "and, please, don't argue about it. I want you to help me. I'm exhausted."

David set to work unwrapping dishes, though by now he had had more than enough of these boxes. They had emptied about four dozen of them, and upstairs they had unpacked about a thousand books and papers and what-nots. And he knew that on the top floor in Mrs. Bartlett's studio there would be, as of this afternoon when Mr. O'Connor had moved her weaving tools, about sixty more cartons with yarns, spools, and records of her business. In addition to which about twenty boxes had to be unpacked in her "office," the front room on the third floor. It would have been nice, David thought, to go to bed before moving and to wake up when it was all over.

The smell of meat and onions frying permeated the kitchen. After a few minutes, Mrs. Bartlett joined him. She opened one of the cartons and started to remove the newspapers that covered the contents. But suddenly she took her hands out and sat down on the floor. "I'm dizzy," she said. "I feel funny," she added weakly. David looked at her. She was very pale and her face was covered with perspiration. The kerchief covering her head had slipped back and strands of hair fell over her eyes. She didn't even push them away. David didn't know what to do. He had never seen his mother in such a state. Her eyes were kind of glassy.

"I'll get you some water," David said. He filled a tumbler at the sink and offered it to her. But she didn't take it.

"Pour it," she whispered. David was so startled that he paused for a second, not knowing what she meant. "Come on—over my head," she said in a choked voice. Carefully David tipped the glass above her head and let some drops trickle down on her. "Come on. . . ." she said again. So David turned the glass upside down. And she just sat there on the kitchen floor, the water spilling down her face onto her blouse and slacks. Then, when David began to laugh—he couldn't help it, she looked so funny—there was a knock on the door and a loud, cheerful voice commanded, "Open up . . . it's me!"

"Grandma!" David yelled. But before he could make his way through the jumble of boxes to the door, Grandma had managed by herself and was standing on the threshold.

Coming from the street, where it was still light, into the shadow-filled kitchen, she squinted. "Who's there?" she asked imperiously. And then, when her eyes became accustomed to the dark, she exclaimed, "For heaven's sake, what a mess! I thought you moved on Saturday. . . ." At last she became aware of Mrs. Bartlett, her daughter, sitting on the floor looking wet and bedraggled, slowly licking the water away from around her mouth. "Jessica, what *are* you doing?" she demanded. "Here, David, take my grips." She handed him a couple of parcels and bags and an old battered suitcase. With a few steps she crossed the kitchen and stood over Mrs. Bartlett, who now was smiling with relief but still didn't talk.

"Jessica, what *are* you doing," Grandma repeated. "Good heavens, did she faint?" she then asked of David.

"I don't know, Grandma," David said. At the same time he realized with a shock that his mother very nearly had fainted.

Grandma shook her head with worry. "I could have told you so, Jessica," she said. "And I wrote you that you would regret it," she added, "buying an old house like this. What you need," she told Mrs. Bartlett, "is a real shower and a nap. Is there a bed made up?" she asked.

"We moved on Saturday," said Mrs. Bartlett, who had found her speech.

"And I can't imagine why you moved at all," Grandma said. "A perfectly nice apartment in a nice neighborhood, and now look at this!" She turned her large frame around and took in the dark kitchen with a sweep of her eyes. "Gloom and doom," she said. "You'd better get up from that floor, Jessica, and take my advice."

"Isn't she wonderful?" Mrs. Bartlett asked of David. She scrambled up on her feet and started to dry herself somewhat with her kerchief. "I so hoped you would come," she said to her mother.

"Then why didn't you ask me?" Grandma inquired. But without waiting for an answer she walked over to the stove and peeked into the pot. "I'll tend to this roast, whatever it is," she scowled. "Of course I take no responsibility, what with that Italian oil you insist on using. However, I'll do the best I can."

"I didn't want to ask," Mrs. Bartlett said, moving toward the door, still drying herself. "I knew you were busy, with classes starting and all that."

"So I am busy, and thank my stars I am, indeed. But I can

spare a few days for you," Grandma snapped, adding in the same breath, "Where do you keep your onions? There aren't half enough in here."

When his mother had left the kitchen, David just stood watching his grandmother. He loved his grandmother. Everybody loved his grandmother, and nobody minded her taking over like that because there was so much affection in her commands. She gave him such a contented feeling, and he had observed that other people always smiled at her and liked to talk to her. When she came for a visit they would move around her in a circle, even those friends of Mother and Dad whom John and Phoebe called "the VIP's" because of their achievements in the arts and sciences. Yes, Grandma was different from other grandmothers, David thought.

Now she stood peeling onions over the pot. She covered the whole big stove with her stout body. Grandma was heavy, all right. Fat . . . as David had told her when he was a little boy. And she dressed in comfortable clothes with wide skirts. Her lovely gray hair was cut short. Everything for comfort, she always said. And her skin was as smooth as that of a young woman, though around her friendly blue eyes lots of tiny wrinkles told you that she wasn't a young woman at all, and that she was past sixty.

"So!" she now said, washing her hands under the faucet. "That's done. It might still turn out to be a pot roast."

"Mother is a very good cook," David said loyally.

"I know. She's good at everything she does," Grandma

said with finality. "Let's sit at the kitchen table. Bring over that lamp there. We'll make some light. And tell me what you've been doing with yourself. How's school this year?" But she did not wait for his reply. "I can't imagine why people want to buy these old houses." This was obviously bothering her a great deal and she couldn't keep her mind off it. "Look at your mother . . . worn to a frazzle already."

"She'll be all right," David said. "And Grandma, it's great to have an old house like this. Do you realize that here, where this house stands, was once Richmond Hill. You know about Richmond Hill, Grandma, don't you?"

"I do and I don't," said Grandma. "All I really know is that it was a beautiful estate in Colonial days, when most of what's now New York City—that is, everything above Houston Street—was just wild country. It always amuses me to think of what New York would be like today if they hadn't taken all the hills down. You know, they leveled it around the beginning of the nineteenth century, don't you? Can you imagine all the mad traffic going up and down steep hills, and all those skyscrapers built on sloping ground?"

"In that case they couldn't have built skyscrapers, Grandma," David said seriously, but then he realized that she was joking and he chided her: "Grandma, you do have the nuttiest ideas."

"I have an imagination," Grandma assented, "and I think I'm blessed for that. Don't you have nutty ideas sometimes?

I hope you do. It makes life interesting. But go on about Richmond Hill."

"Dad told me all I know," David started modestly, "but I mean to do some research on it myself. You see, Grandma, south of where we live now was the land of Lispenard— woods, meadows, valleys, country lanes—oh, you know. Dad said that the Lispenard salt meadows would now approximately be under Canal Street. And you know Canal Street, Grandma. It's mad with traffic."

Grandma nodded. "I do indeed," she said. "An awful street. Too bad humanity never improves on nature."

"Now north of here," David went on, "was the Zantberg. *Zant* is Dutch for sand, *berg* is Dutch for mountain. One hill after the other. Also very fertile land. Richmond Hill stood on a crest, sort of, on the most southerly hill of the Zantberg. That was some neat building. You should see the pictures of it. It had a portico, something like the White House has, and Greek columns—Ionic, they're called—and huge balconies on the second floor. Terrific gardens around it. There was a little lake there, where Minetta Waters ended. That was a stream running through Greenwich Village then. It had lots of fish in it. Trout too, Dad says. And it still runs under the Village, Dad says. Richmond Hill has a real history. George Washington stayed there during the Revolutionary War. He made it his headquarters. And later Aaron Burr lived there. Dad told me that after Burr's wife died, his daughter Theodosia kept house for him. She was only fourteen and she gave those huge banquets. Can you imagine Phoebe running a setup like that?"

"Phoebe lives in a different age," Grandma said. "Phoebe is fine for this age."

"Yes, I know," David said, "but I just can't imagine her doing anything like that. Anyway . . . Vice-President John Adams lived there, too. Oh yes . . . and Burr fought his duel with Hamilton when he lived there. But he never lived there after that."

"He went to England," Grandma nodded. "He had a hard time of it, and when he returned, Theodosia set sail to join him in New York—she had married a southern planter— and drowned. The ship she was on sank off Cape Hatteras."

"I know," David hastened to say. "That was 'The Patriot.'" Then he grabbed Grandma's arm and shook her slightly. "All those things happened and Richmond Hill was right *here*, where our house is, Grandma. I think it's real keen."

"I understand how you feel," Grandma said. "I do, David, I do indeed. It's my worry over your mother. She isn't all that strong, and I know what it takes. I used to run a big house myself. Remember . . . I told you? Over on Washington Square. Your mother was born there." She settled herself on a kitchen chair. But then she got up again to open one of the bags she had brought. She rummaged around in it and came up with a cookie box. "Here," she said. "I baked some of your favorites this morning before train time. It's close to dinner, and I shouldn't." She looked around conspiratorially. "Here, take a few . . . but don't tell your mother I gave you cookies before your dinner."

"Oh, Grandma, I'm almost twelve now. She doesn't care about those things any more."

"I keep forgetting you're growing old," Grandma sighed. "So . . . and how is school?" she asked again.

"Great," David told her.

"Nowadays youngsters like school much better than in my day," Grandma said. "I hated it. I try to teach in the modern way, but I'm too old, I suppose. Still, my pupils make progress and we have fun, too."

"How many pupils have you got this year?" David asked politely.

While Grandma counted on her fingers and mumbled names, David watched her closely and thought how nice it would be to have Grandma live in New York and to take recorder lessons from her, the way John used to. For years she had lived in Boston. New York had gotten to be too much for her.

"I've got nine," said Grandma, who had finished counting. "Three new ones. And two schools."

"Any talented ones?" David was used to having this conversation with Grandma and knew the questions by heart.

"Most children have talent," he was told. David had heard this answer many times before, and he knew what was to follow. "You just have to find it," Grandma said.

"Take a cup of water, David, and add it to the roast," she

told him. "My, I *am* weary," she said. "I wouldn't mind a washup and a nap myself. I haven't even seen the house. However, I promised to watch supper." She put her elbows on the kitchen table and rested her ample chin in her cupped hands.

When David came back to his chair she said, "I know this street from long ago, mind you. Grandpa was born here, in one of those houses across the street. When we were engaged, we used to sit on the stoop on summer evenings. It used to make his parents mad. Such things weren't done in those days. It wasn't proper."

"What was it like then?" David asked eagerly.

"Nice," Grandma said. "Nice, lovely people. Though I remember there was a house across—and come to think of it it might very well have been this very house—where things were not nice. There was an old couple living there then. They were strange. They kept their shutters closed and the children in the neighborhood were frightened of them. Kids used to play all over the street, but never in front of their house. Nobody ever went into the house. . . . They didn't see people, except for a housekeeper. I think she was an Irish woman."

"Was her name O'Connor?" David asked eagerly. "Gee, I bet that it was this house."

"I never knew her name," Grandma said, "but she was Irish."

"Who was Irish?" It was John, coming home. "Grandma!"

he then cheered. "I had a feeling all day that you and I were going to play some duets tonight!"

"Go on, young man," Grandma smiled, "you had no such feelings whatsoever."

"You're sadly mistaken, ma'am," John countered. "There is an invisible microphone in my bosom tuned to your station. I always know what you're doing or where you are."

"Heavens! That should be a nuisance," Grandma smiled affectionately at John.

John, standing behind Grandma with his long arms around her and his hands resting on the kitchen table, rubbed his chin over the top of her head.

"Young man," Grandma said again, "you talk and act as if I were your girl friend."

"You are," John said solemnly. "I am planning to marry you as soon as you reach maturity."

Both Grandma and David laughed, and David thought how close John and Grandma were. David knew the reason for that. When John was small and Grandma still lived in New York, Mrs. Bartlett used to bring John to Grandma on Washington Square every morning before she went to work. Grandma had a great time with John, and it was in her house that he took his first steps and said his first words. She taught John how to play the recorder when he was only three. Right after John entered school she had moved to Boston. She had said at that time that John had been the only reason she was still living in New York, and now that he was taken care of during the day, she was getting out.

It was probably because John had always been so close to Grandma and her music that he wanted to become a musician. He played the recorder and the oboe beautifully.

"Come on, sweetheart," John told Grandma, pulling back her chair, "I'm going to take you upstairs for a rest. You look tired."

"I'm not," Grandma protested, "and I'm watching supper."

"David is a terrific cook," said John. "He'll watch it. Won't you, David?"

"Sure will," David promised.

CHAPTER FOUR

Mr. O'Connor's Story

After the Bartletts had eaten the pot roast, which, as Grandma testified, had turned out beyond all expectations, and after the dishes were done, they again grouped themselves around the table. The cozy light of the table lamp left the rest of the messy kitchen in blessed darkness. Mrs. Bartlett got her notes out to relate the story Mr. O'Connor had told her.

When he was a small boy, Mrs. Bartlett started her tale, Mr. O'Connor's mother was working for an old couple who owned and lived in this very house. Their name was Mac-Laughlin. He remembers that the lights burned all day, because the old couple kept their shutters closed at all times. His mother was the only person who was ever admitted to the house. She had started to work for them when she was only a young girl, and because she felt kind of sorry for them

51

she kept the job even after she got married. She would go there four times a week to clean up and cook their dinner.

Mr. O'Connor remembers that when he was small she used to take him with her. Later she told him that she started taking him to her job shortly after he was born. She kept him in a laundry basket, in the kitchen, because she had to keep him out of sight of the MacLaughlins. They knew he was there, all right, because sometimes they could hear him cry, but they never talked about him to his mother and avoided the kitchen. They never came down anyway. They stayed in their respective rooms and only met in the dining room for their meals. They didn't even talk to each other. Mr. O'Connor's mother never heard them exchange a single word, beyond "Please, pass me the butter," and short sentences like that.

"It ties right in with what I used to hear," Grandma interposed, "so it must have been this house people talked about." She nodded her head with the greatest satisfaction, stroking Porto Rico who had jumped into her broad lap.

"They sound awful," David said. He tried to imagine two people living together without ever speaking to each other. But he just couldn't.

"Quiet, everybody," Phoebe snapped. "Go on, Mommy." Phoebe was hanging over the kitchen table, breathless with excitement. She loved creepy stories. However, she took time out herself to reproach Grandma. "You never told us," she said quickly. "Go on, Mom."

"What was there to tell?" Grandma protested. "We didn't know anything, really. The house was just shut up all the time. That's all. We knew people were living there because, as I told you, we could see lights burning day and night through the shutters."

"There are recluses in every town, small or large," Mr. Bartlett remarked. "Always have been. It's a wonder these people admitted the housekeeper."

"What's a recluse?" David wanted to know.

"People who are afraid of other people. They shut themselves off from the world," John explained.

"There was one room in the house that was never used," Mrs. Bartlett went on, "but the lights were burning there just the same."

"Which one?" Phoebe asked, looking around the kitchen with her shoulders hunched up in suspense.

"An upstairs room," Mrs. Bartlett said. "At any rate, Mr. O'Connor told me that it was a bedroom on the third floor. Oddly enough, Mrs. O'Connor was ordered to change the bed linen once a week, fill the oil lamp, and keep fresh water in the pitcher. He remembers her telling him that she did that for all the fifteen years she worked there. And that the old lady would check up to see whether it had been done, up to the time she was too old and feeble to move from her room."

"Maybe there was a ghost," Phoebe ventured.

"I'm taking Porto Rico to bed with me tonight," Grandmother quipped. "I'm scared green already. Why didn't I stay in Boston, I wonder?"

"Once when he was about eleven years old," Mrs. Bartlett went on, "shortly before the old couple passed away, Mr. O'Connor was allowed to go with his mother when she went to change the bed in that room. During the last year of their lives the old couple never left their rooms any more. They were both served their meals on trays, and at that time his mother went to the house twice a day to take care of them. So after all those years, young O'Connor, who of course had never been permitted to go upstairs, convinced his mother to let him have a peek. She gave in, on condition that he take off his shoes and not make a sound. But the old man must have sensed that the housekeeper was not alone. He came shuffling out of his room onto the landing. Mr. O'Connor still recalls the terror he felt at the sight of that old, old man, with his long, straggly beard and his hair grown way over his collar down his back, standing there and shaking his fist at them. Of course Mrs. O'Connor was used to these strange poeple and their odd behavior, so she just followed her intention to change the bed in the unused room. She went up there and her son followed. Mr. O'Connor told me that he was shaking from head to foot and that to this day he can remember how he literally felt his hair standing straight up on his head with fright. The old man came shuffling up the stairs and into the room, making growling sounds."

Phoebe was clutching her father's hand in fearful antici- pation and whined, "I can't stand it, Mommy. . . . Stop. . . . No, go on. . . ."

David tried to look unconcerned, though something funny seemed to grip at his stomach. And he didn't exactly look forward to going to bed all by himself, goodness knows, maybe in that same room.

Mr. Bartlett and John were chuckling silently, but Grandma gave a loud sigh. "Here I came to spend a few pleasant days with my family, doing some work and spreading good cheer—and look what I got myself into," she said with comic despair. "Gloom and doom! Let's move right out," she ended her complaint.

"What time is it?" David asked, hoping his bedtime would be hours away.

"Did O'Connor tell you exactly which room it was?" Mr. Bartlett wanted to know. He had sensed David's apprehension and wanted him reassured, if possible.

"There are two rooms on each floor, connected by a door. There were always four floors, not counting the basement. The fourth floor was converted into a studio later on," Mrs. Bartlett reminded them. "O'Connor thinks it was the rear room on the third floor."

"Our room," John said philosophically, slapping David on the shoulder.

"I think we ought to have some tea and cookies," proposed Grandma, who felt it was time for a diversion. "Where is my bag?" She winked at David. "I baked some goodies before train time."

Mrs. Bartlett looked up from her notes. She seemed to be

waking up out of a dream. She scanned the faces of her family. "Did I scare you?" she asked innocently.

"Not in the least, dear," Mr. Bartlett answered for them all. But David knew he meant the opposite, and maybe he was even a little annoyed with their mother. "How could you possibly think that?" he added, now openly sarcastic.

"Oh dear, I didn't mean to," Mrs. Bartlett said apologetically.

"Oh, Mommy, go on . . . I can't stand it," Phoebe squealed.

"I'll put the kettle on." Grandma brushed Porto Rico from her lap. On her way to the stove she looked around over her shoulder and remarked with comic resignation, "I must have raised you wrong, Jessica. You are incurably romantic." When she returned to the silent family around the table she shook her finger at Mrs. Bartlett and said sternly, "Your late friend Mr. MacLaughlin was nothing but a nasty old man who hated everybody and was hated in turn by everyone, even his own wife. The rest is poppycock—old wives' tales, and such. This is a very lovely old house, and that's all there is to it, Jessica."

"You just want to unscare us, Grandma," David said, secretly hoping that his grandmother's conviction would be proven true, or would at least put him at ease for the time being.

"Unscare is right," Mr. Bartlett added. "I need unscaring in the worst way."

Grandma dug into her bag, the embroidered cloth bag without which she hadn't ventured out of her house for the last ten years, and proceeded to spread the homemade goodies on the table. There were the cookies David had tasted already and found up to standard, fudge, and a huge poundcake. She also produced something wrapped in tissue paper, which on inspection turned out to be an antique brass door knocker, in the shape of a hand. "That's my contribution to the house," she explained simply.

"Oh Ma, I didn't know you had one like that. I never saw it before," Mrs. Bartlett exclaimed.

Grandma gave her daughter a long look and then sat down in her chair with a plop. "I never . . ." she sighed, shaking her head so vigorously that her soft double chin quivered. For a moment she seemed speechless. Mr. Bartlett and John were very much amused at her indignation, and David realized that his mother's reaction to the gift hadn't been what his grandmother expected.

At last Grandma found her speech, and it came back in a torrent. "Here I've been all over Boston . . . every single antique shop in town . . . to find you a suitable gift, running my poor old legs off for you . . . and you act as if this knocker is something I had lying around in the attic or someplace and . . . and . . . Well, Jessica, I will never never understand your low opinion of what everyone knows is my generosity."

Then both Mr. Bartlett and John burst out laughing, and

Phoebe and David followed suit. They just loved the squabbles between their mother and Grandma, which somehow never made sense and which sounded suspiciously like something put on to amuse the bystanders. If Grandma and their mother were to cease these discussions it would be a sign of something amiss between them.

Mrs. Bartlett quickly got up and hugged her mother. "Thank you very much, darling. It's so beautiful, and just right, and every time I enter the door I'll be thinking of you."

"Nice to know you'll be thinking of me sometime," Grandma said with dignity, taking Mrs. Bartlett's arms from around her neck. "It's a very lovely knocker, Jessica. Seventeenth century, I believe."

"So it is, so it is," added Mr. Bartlett, examing the brass object carefully. "In fact it's a very fine piece."

"Can't we go on now with the story?" Phoebe asked impatiently.

At that point the teakettle whistled and Mrs. Bartlett hastily ducked out from under to make the tea. Grandma cut up the poundcake, and pretty soon they were sitting around having their tea and cake. Mrs. Bartlett asked if it was right to resume her tale.

"You might as well," Mr. Bartlett consented. "But give it straight, will you?"

"Where was I? Oh yes, the old man followed them into the room. As Mr. O'Connor remembers it, it was an ordinary, old-fashioned bedroom: bed, bedside table, chest, cupboard, a table near the window, and two chairs. There was a gas lamp hanging from the ceiling, with the lights on, of course, and a lighted oil lamp on the bedside table.

"As his mother started to take the bedspread off, Mr. O'Connor said he stayed close to her because Mr. Mac-Laughlin was working himself up into a fit of some kind. He was purple with rage, his eyes bulging out of their sockets, and hissing something like, 'Now he won't come back. . . . You did it. . . . You scared him away. . . .' Things like that. He was definitely talking about somebody, but he didn't make any sense. Then he went over to the fireplace and stood in front of it with his arms spread out, as if to prevent anybody from coming near it."

"There is no fireplace in our room," John interrupted calmly. "No fireplace in the back room on the third floor," he repeated.

"You always spoil everything," Phoebe complained, not making much sense.

"Well, as a matter of fact, John is right," Mr. Bartlett began, but before he could say anything else the door from the street slowly, slowly opened, and somebody came through it, standing there in the shadows without saying a word. From where they sat in the circle of lamplight the door opening seemed very dark . . . and the figure posted there darker still. For a few seconds there was a dreadful silence. And when their eyes became accustomed to the dark, they saw an old man with a gray, straggly beard and long gray hair falling over his collar.

"Well, Mr. Bartlett, here I am," he said.

"Mommy! . . ." Phoebe screeched, throwing herself at Mrs. Bartlett, who in turn grabbed her mother's hand. David felt himself getting ice-cold all over. He could hardly breathe, and it took all his courage to remain in his chair. He just grabbed the edge of the table. Several thoughts tumbled through his head at once. So there was a ghost! The old man had come back. And what was going to happen now? He would kill them. Moving here, they had fallen into a trap.

It was the cheerful voice of Mr. Bartlett that broke the spell. "Oh, there you are, Mr. Williams," he said. "I'd forgotten all about our appointment. Come in, Mr. Williams, and would you mind closing the door? I'll be with you in a second." Bending over the table he explained in a whisper, "That's the man who's going to be our janitor."

"Well!" Grandma said in a loud voice. "You could have spared us that much." She folded her arms over her stout bosom and gave Mr. Bartlett a devastating look. "And by the way, don't you people believe in locking your doors? As long as some people don't have enough sense to knock before they enter, it might be a good idea."

"I came home last," Phoebe remembered. "I must have forgotten. I certainly will never forget again, after this. I've never been so scared in my life."

Then Mr. Bartlett brought his visitor to the table and introduced him as Charley Williams, who used to be the janitor for the last owner and would perform the same duties for the Bartletts.

Mr. Williams shook hands all around and sat down in the chair Mr. Bartlett pulled up to the table.

"You sure changed this here building," Mr. Williams said, looking around, appraising the restored kitchen. "Now if you put in another furnace you'll be all set."

"What do you mean?" Mrs. Bartlett asked in alarm.

"Well, I don't want to upset you none, lady, but the furnace in this here building ain't worth a plugged nickel. Them last tenants on the top floor, that painter and his wife, they darn near froze to death every winter. Many's a time they got me out of bed at night to fix it, but what could Charley do? This here furnace is near wore out, and that's the truth."

"Oh no," Mrs. Bartlett groaned. She looked in despair at her husband, who didn't seem to be at all concerned.

"Gloom and doom," said Grandma. "Didn't you check on the heating system?" she asked her son-in-law.

"Don't worry," he said. "It'll be taken care of. I knew the furnace was old, but there wasn't much I could do about it. We got the house at a very favorable price and next year we'll get around to replacing the furnace."

"But you didn't tell me, Carl," Mrs. Bartlett, mumbled, much embarrassed. "I spent all that money on renovations, and if I'd known, I would have . . ."

"I mentioned it," Mr. Bartlett said placidly, "but you didn't even hear me. You were so crazy about the house and wanted it so badly, why should I have wanted to spoil your fun?"

To the amazement of all the onlookers, Mrs. Bartlett got up and hugged her husband. "You are a darling," she said.

David watched his grandmother, wondering what she would think about two grownups who, rather than replace an old furnace, spent all their money on tearing down walls and installing a new kitchen, bookcases, and things. But Grandma just smiled benignly. Then she consulted her watch. "I hope you don't mind, but I want to go to bed. It's been a long day for me. Mr. Williams, will you excuse me?" she asked politely.

Mr. Williams respectfully bowed from the waist. " 'Early to bed, early to rise,' ma'am, that keeps you young."

"We haven't heard the end of the story," Phoebe protested. "Grandma, don't you want to hear the end?"

"Definitely not now," Grandma said. "I'll hear it some other time. There's work to be done tomorrow, and that's what I came for. I want to get a good night's rest."

"There really isn't much more to tell," Mrs. Bartlett quickly told Phoebe. "Mrs. O'Connor just took the old man back to his room. Mr. O'Connor remembers he had to help her support him, because after his extreme anger he kind of collapsed. Afterwards, young O'Connor never went to the house again. He'd had enough. Anyway, Mr. MacLaughlin died about three months later, and shortly after that Mrs.

MacLaughlin was put in a home for the old and infirm and passed away there."

"Then what about that fireplace?" John insisted.

"I guess it was one of those things people think they remember, but they have it confused with something else," Mrs. Bartlett answered.

"You talking about them crazy people who used to live here in the olden days?" Charley Williams inquired. "That story goes way back to Civil War times. I found some letters once when they replaced the old coal bin. Found them in a closet used to be in the furnace room. I got them someplace at home. There's dates on them letters from Civil War times."

Mrs. Bartlett clapped her hands together. Like a little girl, David thought with some embarrassment. "Mr. Williams," she asked breathlessly, "will you bring me those letters? Tomorrow, maybe? . . ." And addressing the whole family she exclaimed, "See . . . who cares about an old furnace? We've got old letters now!"

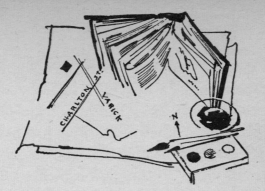

CHAPTER FIVE

Thanksgiving
with an Intermission

However, Mr. Williams didn't bring the letters. He reported that he couldn't find them, but that he was trying hard. He kept coming back with the same message. Whenever he ran into a member of the Bartlett family he would say, "Still looking! . . . Them letters must be someplace, but doggone . . ." and then he would comb his fingers through his unkempt beard and with an honest expresson in his watery old eyes he would promise that any day now . . . After a while it became a joke with the Bartletts.

"I've got a message from Charley," John would begin. "Met him down the block. It's about those letters, you know . . ." and they would burst out laughing, except for David, who could not get his thoughts off the so-called mystery of the house. Frankly, he was uneasy. Those creepy

65

stories of Mr. O'Connor had put a scare into him. For days he hated bedtime. He would never admit it to a soul, but that whole first week before sleep he had crawled way under the covers, just as scared as when he had been a little boy and had believed in goblins and ghosts.

Then one night he had given himself a good talking-to, ordering himself to stick his head out of the blankets and cut out the nonsense. Next day he had started on his intended research on that part of Manhattan which was still called Greenwich Village, to find out for himself what the place he lived in had really been like in the past. With the help of Len, who caught his enthusiasm and who knew his way around the New York museums and libraries, he located the books he needed. They spent hours poring over pictures and maps. They copied them and took notes. After a while David began to get a clear idea of how this part of town had once looked, what kind of people had lived there, and how it all tied in with American history. It made him forget his fears.

David's new hobby had infected most of his class. Even though, as in most New York schools, they had dealt with the subject of New York City when they were eight and nine, they were taking it up again in social studies, this time more thoroughly.

During these weeks the kitchen floor had been turned over with the expected results, Mrs. Bartlett's studio was put into operation, and in general family life resumed its usual pattern. Indian Summer had given way to a raw and rainy fall, and the Bartletts were finding out that Charley Williams had indeed spoken the truth about the furnace at 33½ Charlton Street. Truly, it wasn't worth a plugged nickel. The male members of the family, being of sturdy condition, would put up with it, but the same thing couldn't be said about the female department. Mrs. Bartlett and Phoebe were never encountered without at least one extra sweater over their clothes. Katy Bloomenfield, Mrs. Bartlett's assistant at the studio, was manipulating the pedals of her loom in fur-lined boots. While the temperature on the first, second, and third floors of the house sometimes struggled up to a reading of sixty-five degrees, in the studio on the fourth floor it never reached sixty. And if the day had been especially raw and the furnace had been bullied into some overwork, the invariable result would be a complete collapse on the next day. Then, in the evening, Mr. Bartlett and Charley Williams would have a date in the furnace room, next to the kitchen, where they would work their magic to get the ancient contraption going again. This job would be accompanied by much conversation, which the family could overhear. Lots of "doggone's" from Mr. Williams and much "why don't we's" and "let's try's" on the part of Mr. Bartlett.

The family was extremely permissive and tactful about the whole affair. It was a delicate subject and nobody wanted to rub it in, especially when Mrs. Bartlett was around. Even Phoebe, who was in the sad habit of stepping on people's toes, held her tongue, though she tried to make David the recipient of her complaints as often as he would listen to her.

On the afternoon of Thanksgiving, again she seemed in no mood to hide her discomfort. She had installed herself on the couch in the living room on the first floor with her homework, dressed in a big shaggy sweater, tights, and heavy socks over her slippers. She was wearing earmuffs of soft white fur, which she knew looked very attractive against her dark curls. In the fireplace behind her a nice fire was consuming some logs of pressed wood. These logs were a poor substitute for the real thing, but firewood was hard to come by in the city and very expensive.

Under the mistaken notion that she needed to explain the reason for her costume to David, she said, "*Rigor mortis* is setting in."

On the floor in the middle of the room, David was drawing a map of Greenwich Village in approximately the year 1790, a job he had undertaken with a special purpose in mind. He stopped for a moment and raised himself to his knees. One had to be patient with Phoebe, he reminded himself. Girls that age were impossible, but one had to put up with them. After one of the many fights between David and Phoebe, John had used one of their gabbing sessions before bedtime to explain to David how it was with girls like Phoebe. They were moody but they would outgrow it. One should ignore it. David was willing to give it a try. However, it seemed to him that he had tried for a long time.

"Why don't you go sit in the kitchen?" he suggested. "Mom has the oven going for the turkey. It'll be steaming hot down there. You'll get a free concert in the bargain. Grandma and John are playing. Everybody is down there now."

Phoebe didn't answer. She wasn't going to give up her display of suffering so easily. "The only time I'm really warm is in school," she then volunteered.

"Tough!" David felt all the good will oozing out of him. Even the extra-best intentions, inspired by the spirit of Thanksgiving, were deserting him. "With that fire going it must be a good seventy degrees in here, which is a neat average for any house," he reminded her.

Phoebe ignored that, too. "You know what . . ." she began, "this girl in my class, Andrea Strong, they have this house in Westport. I told her about the cold here and she said she would ask her father if they could bring back a stack of firewood for us after Thanksgiving. She says they have more than they need."

"I bet you've been telling everybody that we are freezing to death in this house," David said with contempt. Then he dismissed her from his mind. He decided to use green paint for Richmond Hill, a small spot on his map, to indicate where once, in the neighborhood of what was now their street and Varick Street, that beautiful estate had been situated.

And after the green had dried, he would take his finest brush and in black would paint two tiny fretted iron posts to mark what had been the entrance to the driveway. Next would be the most difficult job. He would have to shrink Richmond Hill, that massive Colonial building with its porticos, columns, pilasters, and what nots, to the size of a peanut, without losing any of its imposing grandeur. Some job! He made up his mind to first give it a try on a plain piece of white paper, and if he succeeded to copy it off on his map.

The map was important. David and Len had conceived the idea to invite the whole class plus the teacher for a visit to the house and the neighborhood. It would be next week. But before that he wanted to show them his map of Greenwich Village in the olden days, when it was a green and lush country town way north of what was then Manhattan in its small beginning. The map would have to show how rich and fertile Greenwich Village had been long before the subways that rambled underground and the trucks that crowded the streets. The map would show woods and meadows full of game and exotic birds, with the Minetta Brook, with tiny fishermen along its banks. He so wanted to give a clear impression of the hills and valleys of that part of New York before the city had been leveled down. The great estates, the big trees, and all the green and flowers. David was anxious to take his class down to the crowded streets of today. Traffic would be scooting past this way and that way. Trucks being loaded would be blocking the streets. Hundreds of people in a hurry would be crossing at the green lights and disappear into the tall office buildings. And all the while he, David, would know that they first had studied his map of how it used to be. And when he took them to his own house, they would be aware of the fact that on this same spot, way before the MacLaughlins had lived there, around Sixth Avenue and Varick Street, Richmond Hill had stood—that Washington planned his battles there at the beginning of the Revolutionary War. Right here! He hoped he would see in their eyes an expression that proved their brains had made the contact between the old and the today. He wanted them to feel the way he himself had felt when these things had started to click. It made all the difference, David could vouch for that. It had occurred to David that he might become an historian, but he hadn't even mentioned it to Len.

Life had certainly changed since the move to Charlton Street.

This didn't mean that even now he had forgotten about the MacLaughlins and their strange ways. Indeed not. He still wondered why they had acted the way they did. What had made them so loony? Why were they afraid of people? And for what reason was that room on the third floor kept ready, and for whom? Yes, for whom? Once Mr. MacLaughlin had appeared to him in a dream, looking like Mr. Williams and carrying a garbage can out of the house with burning candles on top. Something like a birthday cake. The darndest dream, but not scary.

72

Anyway, he knew now that there were no ghosts in the house. That was a sure thing. It was just a wonderful old house and he liked it.

So . . . the iron posts were done. They didn't look bad at all. And he had managed it without smudging the green.

Next, from his room he would get the library book about Old New York and a sheet of onionskin to trace the picture of Richmond Hill. When he was near the door Phoebe asked, "Where are you going? Don't start anything new. Mom said that the turkey would be ready at four. It's almost that now."

"Stop big-sistering me," David said. But he followed her advice just the same.

It was as warm in the kitchen as David had predicted to Phoebe. Almost too warm. Grandma and John were sitting close to each other on the bench at the kitchen table, like two birds on a perch. On the table, propped up against the festive candle sticks and surrounded by Mrs. Bartlett's best dishes and glasses, stood their music book. But only John was reading the music. As usual, Grandma played by heart, and when Phoebe and David entered she turned all the way around without missing a note. They were just getting to the end of a piece, something slow and old. It sounded lovely.

Mr. Bartlett was sitting opposite them, smoking his pipe and enjoying the music, with a dreamy expression on his face.

Mrs. Bartlett emitted a loud sigh and an "All done. . . ." She heaved the big turkey onto the platter and asked Phoebe to stand by at the stove with the serving dishes.

Grandma took her time with her last long note, all the while nudging John with her elbow to make him drag it out, too, for a whole bar. Then in the next breath she asked Phoebe,

"What in the world do you have over your ears? Going ice-skating?"

Phoebe had forgotten to take her earmuffs off. But when everybody in the kitchen started to laugh, she changed her mind about removing them.

"Now, Phoebe," Mrs. Bartlett exclaimed, laughing in spite of herself, "it isn't all that cold."

"Upstairs it is," Phoebe said, tasting a sprout from the dish she had filled.

Mrs. Bartlett set the turkey in front of her husband and handed him the carving tools. But Mr. Bartlett just held the big fork and knife, ignoring the fowl in front of him for a stern look at Phoebe. "Young lady," he grumbled good-naturedly, "take those awful rabbit skins off your ears and stop making us sorry for you. Enough is enough!"

"I've been thinking," Grandma said, "about that fireplace which O'Connor said was in the back room on the third floor. Not that I want to start that nonsense all over again," she interposed, giving her daughter a look of caution, "but I would think that in a house like this one there must have been more fireplaces than just those two on the first floor. In those days people had no other means of heating their rooms, and who knows . . ."

"They had iron stoves," David reminded her, "or grate fires of Liverpool coal."

"Grandma, you're forgetting that we have an expert in the house." John ruffled David's hair. "Right, Boxhead?"

Mrs. Bartlett sighed. "There's that name again. I thought you had left it in the old apartment, but no such luck. Come on, let's eat. Sit down, everybody, and Happy Thanksgiving."

They took their places around the table and watched Mr. Bartlett carve the turkey. For a moment everyone was silent, but unexpectedly both Grandma and John had their recorders at their mouths and started to play an old Pilgrim hymn. It was a surprise, no doubt about that. Nobody had noticed that they hadn't put their recorders away when they sat down for dinner. After a couple of bars, Mrs. Bartlett's high soprano joined in, Phoebe followed suit, and the next moment David and his father were singing too. Grandma, the practical, stopped playing long enough to tell Mr. Bartlett to go on with the carving so the food wouldn't get cold.

Later, when they were eating the wonderful meal, Mrs. Bartlett asked, "About those fireplaces . . . what did you mean, Ma?"

"Well," Grandma said, examining a piece of turkey on her fork and acting very off-handed about the question, "couldn't there be some boarded-up fireplaces in this house? I wasn't exactly hot on the couch in your office during the night and so I started thinking. Then I got up and tapped the walls in that room, and I wager my helping of turkey . . . by the way, you did a good job, Jessica. It's delicious," she interrupted herself. "I wager my share of the turkey that there is a boarded-up fireplace in your office, anyway."

"Let's go," David shouted, pushing away from the table.

"Take it easy, David," Mr. Bartlett admonished. "We'll take a look after dinner."

"I'm all for taking a look right after the main course," Mrs. Bartlett suggested. There was a glint in her eyes. She couldn't wait herself, but she had a ready excuse for her uncontrollable curiosity. "I took such trouble with the mince pie," she said. "If everybody is dying to go upstairs to tap all the walls in this house, that pie won't be taken as seriously as it should."

Mr. Bartlett started to laugh. "You're absolutely right, Jessica," he chuckled, and to the family in general he announced, "There'll be a ten-minute intermission after the turkey."

And so, after a little while, they all trooped to the third floor, Grandma bringing up the rear huffing and puffing because while climbing the stairs there was another suggestion she found imperative at that moment. "You could use the fireplace as an outlet for a stovepipe. I still have two Franklin stoves in the attic. You're welcome to them."

CHAPTER SIX

Hidden Fireplaces

Mrs. Bartlett might have served canned peaches for all the attention they paid to her mince pie. However, it didn't matter because she herself had forgotten that she had taken so much trouble with it. Her mind was wholly on the discovery they had made on the third floor. There were fireplaces behind the wall, in both the boys' room and the office. And what's more, directly under them, on the second floor, in Mr. and Mrs. Bartlett's bedroom and in Phoebe's room, there were two more.

Mr. O'Connor was exonerated. His memory had served him well.

"I was wondering about fireplaces on the higher floors before we moved in," Mrs. Bartlett said. "But then it slipped my mind," she added. "Didn't you think of it?" she asked her husband.

Mr. Bartlett smiled at her. "Lots of times," he confessed, "but I decided to leave good enough alone. I didn't think we needed them on the upper floors."

"But why were they boarded up, and when?" David wanted to know. "And why did they wall them in instead of just bricking them up and taking off the mantelpiece?"

No doubt he expressed questions the others, too, were asking themselves. Mr. Bartlett furnished the answer. "I suppose that at the time the central heating system was put in, people didn't want their precious heat to escape through the chimneys. So they bricked up their fireplaces, never thinking that in doing it they were taking away one of the characteristic features of an old house and the central focus of every room. Why they walled them in here, I wouldn't know."

"Let's decide which one we're going to open up," Mrs. Bartlett proposed. "Which fireplace, I mean."

So the conversation centered around the job at hand. It was decided that they would open both fireplaces on the third floor, take advantage of Grandma's offer of her old Franklin stoves, and in that way raise the temperature in the upper part of the house.

There was some protest from Phoebe, who didn't think it fair that she be left in the cold instead of the boys. But Mr. Bartlett assured her that in due time they would take care of her needs. It was also decided that the family would use the long Thanksgiving weekend to tackle the job. First thing in the morning, Mr. Bartlett would get the required building material and then the three men in the family would set to work at once. This obviously included David.

"I wash my hands of it," Grandma told Porto Rico, who was ensconced in her lap. "Just between you and me, Porto Rico, I'm sorry I ever mentioned it. They'll wreck the place. And what's more, I came down for a quiet Thanksgiving weekend. The place won't be fit to live in." Porto Rico purred, stretched himself, quivering with the effort, and stuck his claws into Grandma's skirt. As an afterthought Grandma sighed: "I could have eaten a turkey sandwich in a Boston drugstore and wished you a Happy Thanksgiving on the telephone."

While they all laughed, John got up and gave Grandma a good hug. "Don't worry. We'll do a neat job. And we'll move your stuff out of the office into Phoebe's room and put up a cot there for Phoebe. You can stay downstairs till it's all finished, and if anything is amiss you can sue us. Okay?"

But Grandma had to have the last word. "I don't want to sleep with Phoebe. She snores."

Her remark provoked great hilarity. They all knew that Grandma was actually referring to the loud night music she made herself.

And so the next morning the house resounded with the sound of hammer blows. Around ten o'clock there was a hole in the wall of the boys' room just big enough to shine a flashlight through.

"This looks like the real thing," John announced.

"It better be," Grandma commented. She hadn't been able to contain her curiosity and had joined the family, crowded around John.

"What do you see, John?" Mrs. Bartlett asked.

"Nothing much. There is a large recess," John reported. Then he knocked in another hole and another one. Pretty soon he was really swinging the hammer. The family retreated somewhat because plaster flew in all directions. When the cavity was big enough to admit the light of day, and the fireplace became visible, there was a general rejoicing. Mrs. Bartlett and Phoebe did a little dance to express their excitement.

Porto Rico, who from a safe distance had stoically watched the unusual activities, came close for a serious inspection and then suddenly jumped into the ragged hole. They allowed him a few minutes inside, but when he didn't reappear John got impatient and started to bawl him out. At last he made his re-entrance, carrying something in his mouth. It was a crumpled piece of yellowed paper.

"Take it away from him," Mr. Bartlett said quickly, "but be careful about it."

With amazing agility for someone her age, Grandma pounced on the cat, whisked him into her arms, and, oh so carefully, took the wadded piece of paper out of his mouth. She gave it to Mr. Bartlett, who carried it on the palm of his hand. He sat down with it, took out his glasses, and then pro-

ceeded to unfold it, using the very tips of his fingers. They all held their breath. Even though Mr. Bartlett was extremely careful, the edges of the dried-out, brittle paper broke off. "It's part of a newspaper," he said with bated breath.

After a minute more he said, "I've got the date . . . the second year of World War I . . . that's 1915."

"Can you imagine such luck!" Mrs. Bartlett exclaimed. "Now we know when they boarded up the fireplaces." She stared in front of her, to all appearances doing a bit of profound thinking. "In other words . . ." she then slowly said, "in other words . . . old MacLaughlin had that fireplace boarded up just before he died . . . and . . . let's see . . . right after young O'Connor saw this room . . . right after . . ." She didn't finish the sentence, but added, "Remember that O'Connor told me how old MacLaughlin stood in front of this fireplace with his arms spread out . . . as if he wanted to hide it from view? Maybe he was afraid something would be discovered."

"Maybe we'll discover it now," David said hopefully.

"The Lord knows what we'll discover," Grandma sighed with resignation.

"Get me an envelope for this piece of newspaper," Mr. Bartlett asked. "I'll spend some time on it tonight. But now I want to get back to work."

Already, before lunch time, the enclosure around the entire fireplace in the boys' room had been torn down. John had done justice to his reputation as being handier than most boys of his age. Under Mr. Bartlett's direction, he managed the lion's share of the work. David had watched him with admiration and pride. He himself had helped with the removal of brick and plaster, a tiresome and dirty job which entailed much running up and down stairs. Grandma, wearing her hat, against the dust, as she said, had directed traffic on the third floor landing, and in general had told everybody what to do and how to do it.

And now it was done, the floor had been swept, and there was the fireplace in all its glory. It had a wooden mantelpiece with carved panels along its sides. The nicest part was the inside lining of the fireplace—copper plating which, in relief, showed the pattern of the lily of France.

"The fireplace must have been thoroughly cleaned before they boarded it up," Mr. Bartlett said, pointing at the copper lining and the red bricks on the fireplace floor, which, though dusty, didn't show any soot.

But Mrs. Bartlett was quick to remind him that the room hadn't been in use for many years . . . at least, not during the years that Mrs. O'Connor had worked for the MacLaughlins.

Then David suddenly gave a loud shout. "Look what I found!"

It was a drawer in the wall around the corner of the right side panel, just above the baseboard. At first glance, it looked like a piece of wood loosely set into the wall. It was a real coincidence that David spotted it. He tried to open the drawer, but it was stuck.

"Careful . . . careful," Mr. Bartlett, now thoroughly excited himself, shouted.

Everybody talked at once. "Out of the way." "What's in it?" "Let Dad do it." "Let me see, too."

Mr. Bartlett went for his tool box and knelt down by the drawer. After a few minutes, with the whole family standing around him in quiet suspense, a small file did the trick. The drawer jumped open with a little click. "There's a spring in it somewhere," John said, and then, "Oh, darn . . . it's empty."

It was indeed.

"Now what do you think it was used for?" Mrs. Bartlett asked, much disappointed.

Mr. Bartlett looked up at her from his kneeling position. "Think what you would have used it for," he in turn asked her.

"Papers, money, valuables, I guess," she said.

"You bet your life," John added. "Of course, that's where that old nut Mr. MacLaughlin had hidden something he didn't want anybody to know about."

"Maybe he was some kind of crook," Phoebe suggested, her eyes all aglitter. "And he was afraid of the police. . . . That's why he wouldn't let anybody in the house . . . and . . ."

"There we go again," Grandma interrupted. "Let's have

some lunch before we start on the office fireplace. I'm starving."

During lunch, David was very silent. Automatically he ate his turkey sandwich. He didn't even taste it. Something was bothering him. It was a nagging sensation that he could solve the mystery of the drawer. It was something he had read in the library. But what, and in which book? And then, just before his last bite, he jumped up with a "yep," which startled the family.

He ran up the stairs to his room, to his bookshelf, where under a newspaper placed there for protection against the dust and plaster, he found what he was looking for. It was a book on Greenwich Village, a special treasure he had ordered from one of those book-searching firms and paid for out of the pocket money he had saved. Pretty soon he found the page. He just glanced at it, and then ran back down to the kitchen. It was strange, but David felt his hands shaking with excitement. This, he realized, was the way historians would feel when, after years of research, they would suddenly come upon some real find. It might be a date, or a boundary line on a map, or just one paragraph in an old parchment which so far hadn't been noticed by anyone and which now would clarify some mystery or give the key to further research. And now, in his own home, he, David Bartlett, a boy of eleven had most probably found the reason for a drawer at the side of an old fireplace.

"Hey, everybody," he shouted when he entered the kitchen, "listen to this." He put the old volume on the kitchen table and, tracing the paragraph with his finger he read it aloud:

"Richmond Hill had fallen into ruin. It then stood on the line of Charlton Street, some twenty feet from Varick, still wearing the adornment of portico and columns, having been removed there from its old foundations at the intersection of those two streets. In 1849 it was pulled down and they built red brick houses on its grave. In these houses dwelt citizens of quiet and dignified nature, who required their anonymity by the very virtue of their character. However, one of them stood out because of the mystery of his occupation. It has been said that he was a noted smuggler and swindler, though never reached by the long arm of justice."

"Why David!" Grandma exclaimed, full of praise and respect. Out of the corner of his eyes David saw his father and mother look at him with an expression on their faces he would always remember. There was real pride in it.

"Gee," said Phoebe, "how about him!"

"Great work!" John yelled.

"What's so great about that?" David said. "It was in the book and I remembered, that's all." Then, thumping the book, he said, "It *must* have been this house . . . the smuggler's. He must have kept his money in that drawer. . . .

Or do you think that maybe old MacLaughlin had it installed?" he asked his father.

Mr. Bartlett nodded his head. "It's a possibility," he said. "Let's figure it out a minute. O'Connor is about sixty now. He was in this house when he was about eleven. At that time, he said, MacLaughlin was a very old man. Maybe he was eighty. Which means that he died around 1915 and was born around 1835. If we assume that he bought this house when he was about forty, we can set the date of purchase in the year 1875 or thereabouts. No . . . I think your first theory makes more sense. Moreover, this isn't the kind of carpentry they did around 1875. This job dates back to the time when carpentry depended almost entirely on the skill of the carpenter, not on the tools he used. Nothing was done in a hurry; people took time and trouble. Look at the way the sides of this drawer fit together. You can see the dovetails were cut by hand, and look what precision."

"MacLaughlin could have done it himself," John ventured.

But Mr. Bartlett shook his head. "This isn't the work of an amateur. I, for one, would never be able to fit a drawer so neatly into a solid brick wall. As a matter of fact, I think that drawer came with the building, right from the start."

"Then David has a point," Mrs. Bartlett said. "Maybe this was the smuggler's house."

CHAPTER SEVEN

A Loss
and a Find

Though the winter was unusually cold, the Bartletts were comfortable. Even Phoebe had stopped complaining because, along with the old stoves for the third floor, the truck from Boston had brought a small electric heater for her, "with love from Grandma."

They decided that stoves and grate fires were an added attraction. David told his father that next winter, with the new furnace in the basement, he would miss the old-fashioned source of heat in his room. These days, while studying about old New York, he liked to lie on the floor in front of the stove, and pretend that he was living in the times he was reading about.

The visit from David's class had been a success, yet afterwards the other kids gradually lost interest in the subject. But Len and David had become absorbed in the history of

New York during the second half of the nineteenth century. It had started with the suggestion by Len to see if they could find anything more on crooks and smugglers beyond the one paragraph in David's book. So far there had been nothing, but the research was fascinating anyway.

Of course the boys didn't forget about having fun at other things and keeping up with their usual winter activities, like sledding and skating in Central Park when it was possible, Saturday swims in the indoor pool on Thirteenth Street, movies once in a while, theatre and concerts a few times, and their favorite television shows.

That winter the young Bartletts didn't see much of their mother. Mrs. Bartlett was in her studio all day and many evenings. She had been commissioned to do an enormous wall hanging for one of the new air-terminal buildings at Idlewild. Besides Kathy, her assistant, three other weavers had been added for the tremendous job. On the largest loom in the studio, they were weaving Mrs. Bartlett's colorful design of birds in flight and children at play.

Mrs. Bartlett couldn't get over her good fortune. "In the old studio I couldn't have managed it," she would say. "This place is so much bigger." Her studio was indeed. It had been built by a well-known painter less than twenty years ago. It ran the whole length and width of the house with the exception of the small walled-off study for John. And many times she told her husband, "Now I can get the yard fixed up and we'll be able to pay for a complete overhaul of the heating system. Next winter we'll be really warm. Don't you worry."

When she made this same remark on Christmas Day to Grandma, who as always had come to celebrate the holidays, this venerable old lady had a snappy answer for her. "But my dear Jessica, I *am* worried, because if you go on spending your money like you did this Christmas, you won't even be able to pay for fuel. I do appreciate your generosity, though I can't imagine why a woman my age would wear something like this." With these words she eyed the gorgeous Indian wrap her daughter had chosen for her with awe and suspicion.

Mrs. Bartlett had splurged for everyone in the family. David had been presented with his first real watch. It was a man's wristwatch, a Swiss one, thin as a sliver, shock- and water-proof and with a compass added. David finally had excellent use for the little drawer in his room. Up to then it had been empty, because John had his small locked safe for his valuables and David really didn't possess anything he thought was important enough for the cherished secret drawer. But after Christmas he got into the habit of putting his wristwatch in before going to bed, before he went to the pool, or on the days he went ice skating. Then the watch rested in the drawer on a small sample from the weaving studio. It was a fitting treasure for a treasured hiding place, David thought.

One Friday afternoon in February, when he came home from an after-school ball game, the watch was not in the drawer. In spite of being a hundred per cent sure that he hadn't even taken it out of the drawer since he put it there the night

before at bedtime, David looked all over his room. There was always the possibility that Sarah, their cleaning lady, for some reason or other had placed it elsewhere. It went through his mind that maybe she had wanted to scrub the drawer, the way she always cleaned all and everything with a passion, but it certainly was a remote chance. He went up to the studio to ask Mrs. Bartlett whether this had been one of Sarah's days, or whether Mrs. Bartlett had borrowed it for some reason or other.

"Oh, David," his mother said, much disappointed, "I really thought you were old enough now to own a watch." David knew she referred to the Davy Crockett watch he had been given when he was seven and which he first promptly broke and subsequently lost. It made him furious that his mother would react that way. He slammed the door and went back to his room. Losing something like that was the most maddening thing in the world, he thought. It gave you a funny, nagging feeling . . . a helpless feeling, really. And on top of that his mother blamed him. Again he started to look all over. He even inspected the drawer once more. Only then did it occur to him that the woven sample on which the watch rested was gone, too.

"Of all the crazy . . ." David said out loud. "Maybe that nutty Phoebe . . ." he said, and ran out of his room to the landing. "Phoebe . . . Phoebe . . ." he yelled downstairs, "where is my watch? Hey, Phoebe . . . did you see my watch?" It suddenly seemed entirely possible to him that

Phoebe had taken his watch to revenge herself about the night before.

After living in peace for months, they had fought one of their furious fights, all because Phoebe simply wouldn't stop slamming her two doors. The other members of the family had resigned themselves to it, but David, much as he tried, somehow couldn't. Between supper and bedtime, Phoebe had gone in and out of her room at least ten times—either through the door to the landing or through the connecting door to her parents' bedroom—for her endless phone calls, to use some of Mrs. Bartlett's toilet articles, to go to the bathroom, to ask a question of her father, or to look in the encyclopedia in the living room bookcase. And every time there was the loud bang of one of the doors when she left her room, and the equally loud noise when she returned. David had found it impossible to do his homework. Nobody had paid any attention to their screaming insults on the second landing. Mr. and Mrs. Bartlett had chosen to ignore them, and so had John. He had come down from his top-floor study with his school books and had gone past them down the stairs, to finish his homework in the kitchen, without so much as a look or a word.

At breakfast Mr. Bartlett had simply stated, "I trust that this was the last disgraceful spectacle of that kind between you two."

Mrs. Bartlett had added that she hoped people would grow up sometime.

On the way home from school David had wondered why Phoebe could make him so angry. Other people liked her, and she had lots of friends. Nowadays she even had a boy friend —a boy named Terry who went to Irving High in their street. He seemed nice enough and was crazy about Phoebe. Why couldn't he, David, like Phoebe?

He ran down the stairs and knocked on her door. "What do you want?" Phoebe called out.

"Did you see my watch?" David asked around the door.

Phoebe had washed her hair and was sitting before her vanity table rolling strands of wet hair around big curlers.

"No, I didn't," she said. She fastened the curler with two clips and then turned around. "I'm sorry about last night," she said. "I brought you something." She motioned toward a small red book on her bed. "Terry found it in a secondhand book store on Fourth Avenue. He says it is a find. I was keeping it for your birthday, but you can have it now."

"Gee," David said, much embarrassed suddenly. "Gee, that's really neat of you." He took the book and looked at the title. It was called *Introduction to a History of Greenwich Village and Environs*, published in the year 1912. David had never seen it before. If it was in the collection of the Museum of the City of New York, Mr. Farmer, the librarian, had never given it to him. And if the Historical Society or the Public Library owned a copy, both he and Len had missed it. Again he looked at the title page. He noticed that it was published by Davison, a printer in Providence.

"It's a real find," Phoebe said again. "Terry says that it must have been a student's paper, privately printed. I paid four bucks for it," she added.

"I'm going to read it tonight," David told her. "That was really swell of you," he said. Going out of her room he remembered his watch again. "You haven't seen my watch, have you?" he asked, just for the record, because by now he realized Phoebe was innocent. The nagging feeling about his loss, momentarily forgotten because of Phoebe's present, returned. He clutched the book under his arm and went back to his room. Lying on his bed, he tried to trace every movement he had made, every step he had taken since last night. He succeeded in recalling his every action, and it made him all the more sure that he had put the watch in the drawer around nine-thirty the night before and gone to school in the morning without even looking at the secret drawer.

To take his mind off his loss he opened the little red book and started to leaf through it. Within a few minutes he found a vivid description of Richmond Hill and its history. There was nothing new in that—he knew it all by heart—but reading on, he discovered that the Felix Youngman who had written this paper for his doctorate, had done some research on the houses which had replaced the famous estate. The blood rushed to his head with excitement when he read the last page of the chapter:

Among the houses on Charlton Street, the one at No. $33\frac{1}{2}$ is of special interest because of an air of mystery that clung to it during the 1850's. It had been built and was inhabited by Luther Corcoran, an apparently respectable importer of some consequence. However, a number of thieves taken by the police named him as the one who acted as the receiver of their stolen goods. At first the testimony was disbelieved, because of the position said Mr. Corcoran held in the Ninth Ward, but soon the evidence could no longer be denied.

A search warrant was issued and served rather gingerly, but Mr. Corcoran was loud in his protests that the search be carried out with all diligence to clear his name. Nothing was found. However, still further evidence was so incontrovertible that the police no longer acted with such *politesse*, and Corcoran became an object of close suspicion. Subsequent searches of the premises again yielded nothing incriminating, but Corcoran lost some of his previous affability and righteousness.

Nevertheless, the gentleman lived according to a standard that was completely unjustified by the volume of business he transacted in his shop on Pearl Street. It was obvious even to his one-time defenders that there was an unexplained source of income. He then claimed he had inherited from an aunt, but no record of any such relative was ever found.

Even at his death a fruitless search was made of the entire premises. No indictment was ever made against him because of lack of concrete evidence, and the City was reluctant to go into court with only the accusatory word of confessed criminals. Nevertheless, the cloud over his name was never cleared.

David read it through twice. Then he understood the difficult wording of the piece. He jumped off the bed and rushed upstairs to the studio. "Mother . . . I found it . . . look. . . ." He burst into the studio, where everybody stopped working and looked at him expectantly.

"I'm glad you found it," Mrs. Bartlett said. "I was so worried. Where was it? . . ."

Momentarily David was confused by her answer, but in the next instant he realized that she was referring to the watch. It brought him up short. "I didn't find the watch," he said miserably. "But look . . ." He pushed the small red volume toward her with renewed enthusiasm. "Read this!" he said.

First Mrs. Bartlett started reading to herself, but after a moment she called the attention of the weavers. "Listen to this, girls," she said, and read the whole page out loud. The weavers turned around on the bench in front of the huge loom and listened attentively. David realized then that his mother must have talked to them about the house a lot, and that they were fascinated by its history.

When Mrs. Bartlett had finished she said, "Bless Mr. What's-his-name . . ." she looked at the title page, "Felix Youngman. Where did you dig up this book, David?"

"A birthday present from Phoebe."

"Already?" Mrs. Bartlett asked. "Your birthday isn't for another month." Then her face showed sudden understanding. "A peace offering after last night?" she asked.

"Yep," David nodded. He made a face of contrition and spread out his arms in helplessness. "I'm sorry now," he said, "but you know she makes me so mad sometimes."

"I know," his mother said. "You just get on each other's nerves. That's a thing only time will change. Now what about your watch? I'm sorry I was annoyed before, but I thought you had lost it. You didn't, did you?"

"Somebody took it," David said. "Absolutely, Mom. I'm a hundred per cent sure that I put it in the secret drawer last night. Because we'd planned a game in the yard at school, I didn't wear it today. I didn't even open the drawer this morning."

Mrs. Bartlett looked disturbed. "There isn't a soul in this house who would steal a watch," she said. "On the other hand, it doesn't have wings. It couldn't just disappear. So there's something fishy going on. Let's just relax about it until Dad comes home. We'll all look for it." Then she looked at her own watch. "It's five o'clock, girls," she told the weavers. "Let's call it a day. See you tomorrow."

She put a hand on David's shoulder and left the studio with him. Going down the stairs she said, "So, it wasn't a smuggler after all. Just a receiver of stolen goods, Mr. Corcoran was. Kind of dull, isn't it? I still have the feeling that those letters Charley talks about will open new vistas. I think I'll make another foray into the inner sanctum. You want to come?"

"What do you mean?" David asked.

"I'm going to pay a visit on Varick Street," she said. "That's where Charley lives. Tonight!" she added with great determination.

"Can Len come too?" David asked.

"Sure. You'd better do your homework now, before supper," she told him, going down to the kitchen.

"You said 'another foray,'" David remarked. "Have you gone there before?"

Mrs. Bartlett didn't answer.

CHAPTER EIGHT

An Appalling
Discovery

Mrs. Bartlett was really determined to pry those old letters out of the janitor. The page in David's book, and maybe the disappearance of the watch, had given her new impetus. After supper she bundled herself into her coat, put on her galoshes, and wound a scarf around her head.

David had called Len even before he started on his homework. He had shared the excitement of the little red book with him and the maddening frustration about the lost watch. And Len, as a good friend, had come right over, stayed for supper, and had joined in the fruitless search for the watch.

"Where you all going?" Mr. Bartlett asked.

"Visiting," Mrs. Bartlett said with great economy of words.

"Oh, I see," Mr. Bartlett had a deadpan expression on his face, but his eyes were smiling. "Don't take the Coronas this time," he said to his wife. "I've got some nice ten-cent cigars in my closet. Second shelf from the top."

Mrs. Bartlett started to giggle. "You're quite a detective, aren't you?"

"A man has to defend his property," Mr. Bartlett said, going back to the evening paper he was holding.

Len and David looked at each other and shrugged their shoulders. They didn't get any of that conversation, but then, that's how it was with parents. Sometimes they talked in riddles and you did know better than to ask for an explanation.

"Come on, boys," Mrs. Bartlett called, "let's go. . . ." and she marched out of the door.

David and Len quickly went for their jackets and ran after her. They caught up with her at the corner of Varick Street. She was hurrying along through the slush that covered the New York sidewalks. With the exception of a couple of taxis and a private car which was proceeding slowly up the messy street, the thoroughfare was deserted. With all the offices, factories and warehouses closed for the night, there wasn't a pedestrian around and no trucks in sight.

"I've been patient enough," Mrs. Bartlett told the boys. "Either Charley has those letters or he hasn't, but I'm going to find out one way or the other. I'm sure those letters, if they exist, will give us the clue to the history of the house. With the story of the smuggler reduced to just a dull report on a crook, I think we've got to find more on the MacLaughlins. I bet Charley's letters will put us on the right track. Well, here it is. . . ."

She stopped at an old brownstone building, one of the few that hadn't been torn down to make place for the tall structures of commerce.

"Do we go up or down?" Len asked. He had stepped to the edge of the sidewalk to take a good look at the dilapidated building. David joined him. There were six floors. The first three, as the lettering on the windows indicated, housed offices and small factories. A dentist and chiropractor operated on the first floor.

Lights were burning on the three floors above. The windows were curtained. "Can you imagine climbing all those stairs?" David asked.

But Mrs. Bartlett was going down the stairs to the basement. "Come on, fellers," she called.

There was a sign across the two boarded-up basement windows which read:

C WILLIAMS
CARTS FOR RENT
50 CT. HOUR
CISORS AND NIVES
CHAR PENT

"A little sideline," Mrs. Bartlett smiled, pointing to the sign. "Charley is an industrious fellow."

She knocked on the rickety door. A dog started to bark furiously inside, and they heard the voice of Charley telling

the animal to take it easy. Steps approached the door and Charley inquired, "Who's there?"

After Mrs. Bartlett had identified herself, a series of bolts were moved from the inside, a rusty key ground in the lock, and Charley peeked his head around the door.

"It's no use, ma'am," he said. "If I stoke her up, she'll die on me tomorrow. And as it being a Sunday the next day . . ."

"I didn't come for the furnace, Charley," Mrs. Bartlett assured him. "We came to bring you a smoke for the weekend. Can we come in?"

Charley opened the door wider. He was dressed in an extremely dirty suit of long underwear and he carried a flashlight. The dog, wagging a ragged tail, sniffed busily to get acquainted with the visitors, then, satisfied with the result, disappeared into the darkness of the apartment.

From her coat pocket Mrs. Bartlett produced two of Mr. Bartlett's ten-cent cigars and put them in Charley's hand. For an instant David wondered whether she always carried cigars in her pocket, just in case, but then he remembered the mysterious conversation between his father and mother before they left the house.

"Why, that's right nice of you, Mrs. Bartlett," Charley said. "I still have one left from the other time. But I haven't found the letters, ma'am," he added shrewdly, shaking his head. The beam of light slid back and forth with the movement of his head and gave quick glimpses of four pushcarts, neatly parked side by side in Charley's front room.

"We came to help you find them," Mrs. Bartlett said resolutely, and moved away from the front door toward the back of the apartment. "Don't you have a light here, Charley?" she asked, followed by a "Heavens . . . ouch . . ." because she had obviously bumped herself.

"Ran out of bulbs," Charley said. "Just a minute, ma'am." The flashlight came forward and led the way to the back of the house. David knew that Len, next to him, was laughing, but he himself was getting embarrassed. However, he followed the beam of light through another small room full of mysterious shapes, around a corner, into the sudden light of Charley's kitchen. This, apparently, was the place where Charley lived, slept, and cooked. It was in an indescribable mess. It looked more like a junk shop than living quarters. However, near the oven Charley had made a cosy corner for himself with an old-fashioned wicker chair with some greasy pillows on it, a rickety floor lamp, and a magnificent television set of recent vintage. The set was on, but there wasn't a sound out of it.

"What a lovely set, Charley," Mrs. Bartlett said, pulling off her woolen mittens and looking around for a place to sit down. Charley grabbed some garments piled on top of his small icebox and left the kitchen for a moment.

"Mother," David whispered, "let's go. You just can't . . ."

But Mrs. Bartlett interrupted him. "I've been here twice before to try . . ."

"With cigars," Len added.

"Apple pie the first time, cigars the second time," Mrs. Bartlett went on imperturbably. "Never got beyond the front door. This time I won't leave without the letters," she said grimly.

"You never told us," David reminded her.

"Who wants to talk about failures?" said Mrs. Bartlett. She sat down on the greasy pillows.

Charley returned. With his clothes on he had regained his composure. He seemed to enjoy the visit and started to bustle about the stove for "a hot cup of coffee."

"That sure is a nice little set," Charley concurred, taking up the conversation where he had left the room. "It has a nice sound, too. But I don't take with the sound. The pictures are enough for me. They always say the same things, anyways."

"Those are golden words, Charley," said Mrs. Bartlett, who hated television and refused ever to look at it.

"It's a classy set," Charley said. "I bought me that only the other day. I've got a little business on the side," he explained.

"I noticed that," Mrs. Bartlett said. "You painted that sign yourself?" she asked.

Charley shook his head sadly. "I don't spell so good, ma'am. But my little nephew—he's only seven, but he's got a real head on his shoulders—he painted that there sign. Anyways, that's not the business I was talking about. I'm kind of an importer. I sell stuff for the sailors who bring me goods from the other side. Yardgoods, cigarettes, watches—lots of things. It saves on import duty and taxes. It ain't crooked and it ain't straight," he winked at Mrs. Bartlett, "but a body has to make a living. Want to buy a nice little watch, ma'am?" he then asked. He opened one of the stove drawers, in which less adventurous people keep their frying pans and other cooking utensils, and took something out. "Nice little watch . . . Swiss import," he said appraisingly, dangling it by the strap in front of Mrs. Bartlett.

When David saw the watch he gasped, and was about to grab it, but Mrs. Bartlett got it first. She gave David a warning look, and admiring the timepiece she said, "A nice little watch indeed, Charley. How much would you sell it for?"

David came to stand behind his mother to make quite sure that it was his watch. If it wasn't, it surely was an incredible coincidence. David felt quite sickened by the discovery, and at the same time, in a strange way, frightened. Len just shook his head, but he didn't say a word. He just watched Mrs. Bartlett.

Charley started pouring coffee in the big white mugs he had taken from the top of the stove. "I might let that go for twenty dollars," he said. "A special price for you, Mrs. Bartlett," he added.

"I'll tell you what I'll do," proposed Mrs. Bartlett. "If you will let me, I'll take this watch home to my husband. If it's all right with him to buy it, it's a deal. All right, Charley?

It would make a nice little Christmas present for David," she said.

At this point Len came out with a sound that was a cross between amazement and admiration. David knew just how he felt. The way his mother was handling the appalling discovery was astounding.

"David is a fine young gentleman," Charley said. "He deserves the best. Even though Christmas is dead and gone," he then joked.

Mrs. Bartlett put the watch in her coat pocket. "I'll let you know very soon, Charley," she said. "Now . . . about those letters—where do you think they could be?"

"They're in the back parlor," Charley told her. "That's a fact. But inasmuch as I use that there room for my business —storage, you know—it's kind of difficult."

"I bet it is," said Mrs. Bartlett, in a most understanding way. "This is good coffee, Charley. I needed that." She winked at David and Len, who were still standing around completely at a loss as to how to act. David would have liked to get out of the place as fast as possible, and he was sure Len felt the same way, but his mother didn't seem to want to. She was sitting on the greasy pillows of the wicker chair, sipping her coffee, completely at ease. She's after those letters, David thought. She might want to go to the police about the watch, after which she wouldn't have another chance at those letters.

"I'll make you a proposition, Charley," she said. "Len and David will go back to the house to get a light bulb and a couple of flashlights. Then we'll all search for those letters in your back parlor."

"That's real kind of you, ma'am," Charley said, shaking his head to indicate that not many people would be as kind as Mrs. Bartlett, which was a truly amazing fact to contemplate. "But it's late, Mrs. Bartlett. It's near nine o'clock . . . Charley's bedtime. Inasmuch as I got to get up at the crack of dawn for that doggone furnace of yours, ma'am—if you don't mind me saying so—I'd better turn in now."

At this point there was a loud knocking at the front door. Again the dog barked.

"I sure am popular tonight," said Charley, and shuffled off to the front.

"Let's get out of here, Mom," David whispered. "That guy is a thief and a crook. You know he stole my watch. What do you want to sit here for?"

"There are a lot of imported Swiss watches of the same make," Mrs. Bartlett whispered back. "You don't know for sure. Remember, a person is innocent until he's proven guilty. Charley isn't the type to steal from people. And at any rate, I want those letters."

Then they heard the voice of Mr. Bartlett at the front door. "Are my wife and son here?" he asked. "It's awfully dark in this neighborhood, so I came to pick them up, Charley."

The expression on Mrs. Bartlett's face turned from determination to delight. And when Mr. Bartlett walked into the kitchen she gaily waved at him.

"Join the party," she said. "We're just getting ready to search for those letters. Len and David are going back to the house to get a light bulb—Charley is all out of them—and a couple of flashlights, and then we'll go into Charley's back parlor and find those letters." She emphasized the word "find," and Charley, who had followed Mr. Bartlett into the kitchen, seemed to realize that he might as well throw in the towel and go along with Mrs. Bartlett's plan. "That's what we was just going to do," he told Mr. Bartlett.

When David and Len hurried back to the house for the flashlights and bulb, Len said, "Your mother should have lived in the time of the pioneers, or something. Boy, she's got guts!"

"It'll give me the creeps to go looking for things in that filthy place," David told him. "Mom never minds those things. When we bought the house, remember how dirty and neglected it was? Those roomers left the worst mess, and she just went in there and cleaned it all up. And anyway, I hate to touch anything that belongs to that guy, the dirty, thieving crook. I've got to tell Dad the minute I can get to him."

"Relax," said Len. "I know it looks like he did steal it, but on the other hand I can't believe it. He doesn't seem like a thief to me. Of course, he has these deals on with the sailors. They smuggle the stuff in for him, I guess, but that's still

different. I bet he doesn't steal things from the people he works for, just as your mother said."

"You know so much," said David, but at the same time he felt that Len might be right.

Searching for the lost letters in Charley's back parlor was indeed not a job for squeamish people. The shapes they had noticed in passing through that room proved to be all kinds of cast-off articles which Charley had accumulated in the hope of some day selling them. Broken-down perambulators, discarded sewing machines, rusty car engines, old pieces of furniture, and at least ten moldy trunks and satchels of days gone by. It was toward the trunks that Charley directed their attention. He had an enormous bunch of keys, most of which might well have been used to unlock the gates of

medieval castles or ancient prison doors. They were huge and rusty and, as Mrs. Bartlett quickly noticed, hand-wrought antiques. Charley felt very important about them and put on quite a show, rattling them, squinting at them, and wasting everybody's time with them. In the end the trunks had to be pried open with file and hammer, a job which had Mr. Bartlett in a big sweat. But at last they could examine the contents.

Most of the trunks were empty or filled with rags and garments in an advanced state of deterioration. There was one, a Saratoga trunk, filled with old family pictures, some daguerreotypes among them. Charley told Mrs. Bartlett that he had bought "the lot" at an auction, and she offered him five dollars for them.

Good salesman that he was, Charley said "six." And Mr. Bartlett wanted to know what in the world she wanted with them.

"Oh, Dad," David exclaimed, "don't you understand? . . ."

Mr. Bartlett quickly said that he did, and dug into another Saratoga trunk which was filled with papers. There were rolls, bundles, and stacks of them.

"That's her," Charley informed them. And after all the months of postponements, he now declared, without moving a muscle or a sign of embarrassment, that he remembered "as if it was yesterday" that some fifteen years before he had put the letters found at 33½ Charlton Street, "in that there trunk."

Just to be on the safe side, Mrs. Bartlett inspected every one of the wardrobes, but none of them contained papers. At her request, Charley produced a gunny sack, the pictures and papers were stuffed in, and after fond goodbyes from both sides, the Bartletts and Len departed for home.

As soon as they got out into the street, David told his father about the watch. Since his talk with Len he was even more torn between the conviction of Charley's guilt and knowing that Charley was just a funny old man but not a thief. On the other hand, the watch had been taken out of the drawer. There was no doubt about that. "And Dad, I recognized it by the band. That's exactly the same, too," he ended his story.

"Those watches come with that kind of band, David," said Mr. Bartlett. "As soon as we get home I'll make sure."

"How can you?" David asked.

"I have a way of telling," was the answer.

When they got home they set the heavy sack on the kitchen floor and Mrs. Bartlett handed her husband the watch from her pocket.

"Give me your wrist, David," Mr. Bartlett asked. David extended his arm and Mr. Bartlett put the watch on his wrist and fastened the clasp. "Now, will you all take a good look," he said. Mrs. Bartlett bent over David's wrist and said, "What a relief!" Len looked and said, "I knew it." And David took a look, shook his wrist, and said absolutely nothing. But inwardly he apologized to Charley for suspecting him.

Mr. Bartlett had closed the clasp on the band to fit tightly around David's wrist, but the mark on the band showed that the watch had been worn by someone with a much broader wrist than David's. "As you all can see, for David the watchband closed on the third hole," Mr. Bartlett said, "and the person who wore the watch before used the first hole. He must have been a big man."

"Probably the sailor who smuggled it into the harbor," said Len.

"Carl, you could be another Sherlock Holmes," said Mrs. Bartlett with much admiration. "But where is David's watch?" she sighed.

"The watch will be found," Mr. Bartlett assured her. "You'd better get this one back to Charley first thing in the morning." Then he started to laugh. "Jessica," he said to his wife, "if I'm Sherlock Holmes, you could be Watson. And now let's wash up a little and get to work on the papers." Then he turned to Len. "I suppose you want to be in on the fun. Why don't you call home and ask if you can spend the night? John's gone up to Boston. . . . You can sleep in his bed."

Much pleased, Len made for the telephone and Mr. Bartlett, after his turn at the sink, piled all the papers on the kitchen table.

CHAPTER NINE

"Dear Brother . . ."

There were stacks of household accounts and business ledgers, rolls of bills, and many bundles of letters.

First Mrs. Bartlett separated the letters from the rest of the papers. "It's a shame John and Phoebe are away. They'll miss all the fun," she remarked.

"Listen to this," Mr. Bartlett exclaimed. He had opened one of the household books and read aloud: " 'Washing, 97¢.' (I bet that was a stack of laundry as tall as I.) 'Turnips, 3¢, side of beef, 37¢.' Those were the days," he sighed. "In 1885 you could really live cheaply."

Mrs. Bartlett took a worn and faded pink ribbon off a bundle of letters. "Come on, now," she said. "Let's each read one bundle."

"But how will we recognize the ones we're looking for?" asked David.

117

"That's a good question," Mr. Bartlett said. "We're looking for letters written to MacLaughlin. The ones in the envelopes are easy enough—they should have the MacLaughlin address. The ones without should be written to Joseph. That was his first name."

"What was his wife's name?" Len wanted to know.

"Catherine." Mrs. Bartlett was reading a yellowed letter, written in a spidery hand. "This is one to Angela, 'My dear Angela,' " she read, " 'I'm delighted to hear that you have recovered your health . . .' "

"Hang Charley," said Mr. Bartlett grimly. "Why did he have to throw our letters in with these?"

"Because he's a very orderly man," Mrs. Bartlett giggled.

"Yikes," Len exclaimed, "listen to this one." With much difficulty, he read, " 'My love, I waited for your maid at the corner. She vowed she would hand my note to you. We must abide by your father's decision. But one day, upon my honor, I will convince him that I am worthy of you, my darling Angela.' " Len looked up, grinning rather sheepishly. "Shall I go on?" he asked.

"Not for me," Mr. Bartlett said quickly. "I bet all those letters belonged to 'My Darling Angela.' She saved every scrap of paper that concerned her . . . even her household ledgers. What's the date on that letter, Len?"

"January 16th, 1869."

"My bundle runs from 1882 to 1883," Mrs. Bartlett reported. "What luck that we found all those papers. Later on, when my wall hanging is done, I'm going to have a great time with these letters. There'll be the whole story of Angela's life. But now let's concentrate on finding ours. Remember, we're looking for the names Joseph and Catherine Mac-Laughlin. Just put the 'Angela' ones in the middle of the table."

They were all silent for a while, giving all their attention to the search. At one point Mr. Bartlett remarked that the art of correspondence was a lost one.

"I hate to write letters," Len told him, "and I can hardly read these."

Then David gave out with a yelp. "I think I've got one," he shouted. "Listen—

" 'Dear Brother. . . .' This letter was written from California in 1869," he interrupted himself.

" 'Dear Brother,' " he began again, and slowly he read, " 'after three years of arduous labor I finally struck pay-dirt. I'll be leaving here in a few days from now & expect to be in New York before the summer. Your mail will not reach me on the way & since I gather from your last letter that you intended to buy a house, I beg of you to leave your new address at the offices of Wells Fargo in New York. My respects to my new sister-in-law, your wife, whose acquaintance I am impatient to make. Yours, as ever, William.' "

Mrs. Bartlett clapped her hands, indicating that she had reached the peak of excitement, but Mr. Bartlett was still a bit skeptical and said, "Tut tut, hold your horses, dear. The world was full of Williams who wrote to their brothers from California. This one struck gold—that's what pay-dirt meant. Let's see—1869. The original gold rush in California was twenty years past, but new discoveries were still being made. Maybe we can find another letter in the same handwriting." He scanned the table and pushed some bundles of letters around. "Yes, by gum," he then said, and reached for a single yellowed envelope, which bore the same masculine script. The envelope showed no postal stamp and had obviously been delivered by hand. After a tense moment he nodded his head with great satisfaction. "Yes . . . we seem to have hit the mark," he announced, and held the envelope up so the others could read the address: "Mr. Joseph MacLaughlin, 33½ Charlton Street, New York City."

While he pulled a sheet of paper from the envelope, Mrs. Bartlett, David, and Len watched him breathlessly.

" 'Joseph,' " Mr. Bartlett began:

" 'Pray, assemble my possessions, such as you did not think worthy of stealing too, & hand them to bearer of this note. I have finished with you forever. You are a thief & a lout. Your protestations have fallen upon deaf ears. Your offer to call in the police is all the more proof of your brazen deceit & be damned to you. I pity your wife, Catherine. I know she is innocent. I am leaving this town for good.—William.' "

"Wow!" David exclaimed. "What happened?"

Mr. Bartlett reread the letter silently. Then he handed it to Mrs. Bartlett, and while she and the boys read it again

he took out his pipe and tobacco pouch and, deep in thought, proceeded to prepare for a smoke. "I suppose our friend Joseph MacLaughlin grabbed brother William's stake," he then said. "That's an old story. Gold did strange things to people."

"What a lousy thing to do!" David said.

"Here's another one," Len cheered, holding up a third envelope addressed in the same handwriting. From it he removed two letters, one in the now familiar bold writing and another one, a business letter, in an almost illegible slanting scrawl.

"Read that one first, Len," Mr. Bartlett asked, pointing with the stem of his pipe to the business letter.

" 'Dear Sir,' " Len began. "I can hardly read it," he said, squinting at the paper. "Some scrawl . . . 'Summoned by your brother, Mr. Joseph MacLaughlin, & at his request, my assistants and I made a thorough search of the premises at 33½ Charlton Street, residence of the aforementioned gentleman, & at his urgency am reporting to you that no trace was found of the missing gold contained in linen sack deposited in drawer as per your claim. . . .' "

"See . . ." David interrupted, shouting so loud that his mother held her ears, "see . . . he used my drawer. . . ."

"Go on, Len," Mr. Bartlett said.

" 'Since upon examining doors, locks, and window latches, as well as soft soil at entrance from garden door, we found no sign of breaking & entry, we are pledged to pursue our investigation for Mr. Joseph MacL., who, by the by, was never actually shown the aforementioned gold & has no proof of its existence. To facilitate the aforementioned investigation, we request your presence at the interrogation of witnesses tomorrow at 10 a.m. o'clock on the aforementioned premises.—Respectfully yours, Charles Flower, for Allan Pinkerton, Chicago.' "

Mr. Bartlett slapped the table, grinning broadly. "This is fabulous," he shouted. "Joseph called the Pinkertons on the case!" When he saw the puzzled faces of his wife and the boys he explained, "Allan Pinkerton was the first 'private eye' in this country. He is said to have thwarted a plot to assassinate Lincoln back in 1861. He worked out of Chicago." Mr. Bartlett chuckled. "That Joseph certainly was on the ball. A man ahead of his time, to call in a private detective in those days."

Len and David were punching each other with excitement and Mrs. Bartlett could barely contain herself.

"You know the Pinkertons," Mr. Bartlett went on. "Those uniformed guards at banks and museums and auctions and such . . . that's still the same firm." Mr. Bartlett shook his head in amazement. "It's pretty fantastic," he said. "This story is getting better all the time."

"The other letter," David suddenly remembered, and he grabbed it from the table in front of Len. "I'll read this one." He unfolded the sheet of paper. "It's from William, of course," he reminded them. " 'J.'—just J.—he's really mad now. 'This piece of drivel by one of your henchmen was forwarded to me by my New York agents, where it was left after my departure. I am returning it to you as proof that "the aforementioned" gentlemen were worthy of your confidence. Keep it for the day of the "pay-off." I am truly impressed by the company you keep.—William.' That's one I don't understand at all," David said.

"What's the postmark on the envelope?" Mr. Bartlett asked.

David inspected the envelope. "St. Louis," he told his father. Mrs. Bartlett looked over his shoulder. "Yes, St. Louis," she said. Then she sighed in sympathy. "The poor guy was probably on his way back to California to start all over again. But he did have a sense of humor," she added. "Aforementioned struck him as funny, too. Did he add quotation marks? Let me see the letter, David. Yes, quotation marks," she said smiling. "I knew he was being facetious."

"What do you mean? I don't understand that letter," David said again.

"I don't, either," said Len.

"William didn't hold a high opinion of detectives," Mr. Bartlett explained, "which is only logical, because in those days they were virtually unknown. He thought that the man from Pinkerton's was hand in glove with his brother and would be paid off for declaring that Joseph was innocent and that there had never been any gold in the house.

"The way I reconstruct it is that William came to the

house with his pay-dirt, the gold he had found in California. He arrived too late to deposit it in the bank, and Joseph, to whom he mentioned it, advised him to store the gold in the drawer. The next morning the gold was gone and William accused his brother. Joseph was either innocent, or, as William called him, 'a lout and a thief.' Whichever, Joseph either was so sure that he wouldn't be found out, or was so entirely guiltless, that he called on Pinkerton to find proof. But William didn't want any part of it. I suppose there must have been reasons that William suspected his brother so readily. Maybe they didn't get along when they were younger. And come to think of it, it was rather strange that one brother could afford to buy a house and that the other had to go out west and dig for gold. And, of course, stranger still that the gold should disappear overnight."

"Now I understand why Joseph became a hermit," Mrs. Bartlett said. "If he was innocent, it was enough to drive him half mad and make him retire from the world. And if he stole the gold, he must have been hounded by his own guilt feelings. And maybe his wife didn't trust him. Remember, Mr. O'Connor said they never talked to each other. She must have been the kind of person one couldn't possibly suspect of duplicity. William wrote in his second letter that he knew she was innocent. That in itself must have been awful. And now I understand why they held that room ready. Joseph kept hoping that William would come back. And I suppose later on he became superstitious and thought that if the room was kept ready, William would come back."

"It certainly was a dreadful situation," Mr. Bartlett mused. "Just think of it. And I suppose that they were never reconciled and that the mystery was never solved. Let's just make sure that there isn't any other correspondence. Charley never told us how many letters he found."

Again they searched among the papers until all Angela's mail was piled in the middle of the kitchen table and the job was done.

"That's it, then," Mr. Bartlett said. He yawned and looked at his watch. "Time for bed," he announced. "Come on, boys, it's way past your bedtime."

Automatically, David moved his arm up to check the time. When he saw his bare wrist he remembered his loss. In the excitement he had completely forgotten.

Mrs. Bartlett had noticed his gesture and the subsequent expression of disappointment on his face. "What about David's watch now?" she asked her husband.

"First thing tomorrow morning the boys had better go back to school and make sure the watch wasn't left there. The janitor will let you in, won't he, David?"

"But Dad—I didn't take it to school," David protested. "I swear I didn't."

"I know," Mr. Bartlett said kindly. "I know, feller. Just the same, I want you to make absolutely sure. Unless we are certain, I can't question people about it. It's darned unpleasant, anyway." He looked at his wife with a frown. "Jessica,

I'd hate to do this . . . but if the watch doesn't turn up, I will have to question your people in the studio."

"Oh, Carl," Mrs. Bartlett wailed, "that's awful. They're such nice girls, and I know they wouldn't take a thing from anybody."

"How about John?" David burst out. "I never thought of it, but maybe he took it to Boston, because his watch broke or something. Can I call him at Grandma's?"

"Go ahead," Mr. Bartlett told him, but the expression on his face showed that he didn't expect much to result from the call.

"Tell them about the letters. . . ." Mrs. Bartlett called after David when he was on his way upstairs.

David was back in a few minutes. "I woke them up," he said. "No . . . John doesn't have it." Then David smiled. "Grandma said to tell you that you won't have a minute's peace until you sell this house and move into a sensible apartment. She also said that we're ruining our health by staying up till all hours."

"I knew she would," Mrs. Bartlett said resignedly.

CHAPTER TEN

Two Sunday Afternoons

That weekend David was alone with his parents. Saturday morning Len had accompanied him to school, a mission which had proven useless, and then went home. Phoebe had decided to extend her overnight at a girl friend's house into two overnights. And John was still in Boston, where he had gone to assist Grandma with her yearly students' concert, an event which never took place without the participation of Grandma's star pupil.

It hadn't happened in a long while that David was alone with his parents for more than a few hours at a time. He couldn't even recall the summer, of which Mrs. Bartlett tried to remind him, when John and Phoebe had spent their vacation at Grandma's and he had been too little to be away from home for so long.

David enjoyed being the only child in the house, and apparently Mr. and Mrs. Bartlett didn't mind it, either. They had proposed a Sunday program of a leisurely late breakfast, an afternoon jaunt to the Metropolitan Museum, and dinner out.

On Sunday afternoon when they got off the Fifth Avenue bus at Washington Square, they bumped into Mrs. Hough, "the lady downstairs." They hadn't seen her since they moved from her building. At that time mutual feelings hadn't been too cordial, and David suddenly remembered how his mother had blown her a happy farewell kiss when she moved out of the building. However, the passage of time had rounded the sharp edges, and the reunion was nothing short of friendly. "The lady downstairs" said a "Well, what do you know. . . ." and beamed. Mr. and Mrs. Bartlett smiled recognition and promptly inquired after the lady's well-being. They were told that this left nothing to be desired, whereafter Mrs. Bartlett, with a mischievous glint in her eyes, wanted to be informed on the progress Mrs. Hough was making in her piano studies.

"I've often thought what nice tenants you people were," she answered. "The people I rented the place to after you left were a perfect nuisance. They stamped on the floor when I practiced for more than two hours, and once they even called the police when I played after midnight."

Mrs. Bartlett could hardly keep a straight face about the belated compliment, and Mr. Bartlett had a sudden coughing fit, which made him politely turn his back. But David just grinned. That Mrs. Hough surely didn't know the score.

"The lady downstairs," who didn't seem to have urgent business elsewhere, sauntered along when the Bartletts took a course homeward. Pretty soon the conversation centered around the advantages of having a house of your own.

On being informed that the Bartletts now owned a building on Charlton Street, Mrs. Hough nodded approval, but when she learned that it was number 33½, she reacted in an unexpected way. "Oh no, not that house!" she called out. After this outburst she became very serious. Kind of sad, David thought. She said, "33½ Charlton Street just about ruined my childhood!"

The three Bartletts felt that something really bad had happened to Mrs. Hough in connection with their house. For a moment they didn't know what to do, but then Mrs. Bartlett placed her hand under Mrs. Hough's elbow and managed to put some distance between the two members of her family and herself and her companion.

"Do you want to talk about it, Mrs. Hough?" David overheard her asking. But "the lady downstairs" just shook her head, and David, walking with his father a few paces behind, noticed that it was quite a while until she was able to talk again. When she finally did, she spoke rapidly and at great length. They reached the corner of Sixth Avenue and King Street before she came to the end of whatever she was telling Mrs. Bartlett. By that time Mrs. Bartlett and Mrs. Hough seemed the closest of friends, and David was furious.

"What a dirty trick of Mom's," he confided to his father. "I wanted to hear the story too."

"Watch your language," Mr. Bartlett said, and added, "Your mother is a very sensitive person, David. Mrs. Hough was obviously very upset and your Mom noticed it and gave her her sympathy." After a moment's silence he remarked, "It seems to me that just about everybody is in some way or another connected with our house."

When Mr. Bartlett and David caught up with the two women, Mrs. Hough was saying, "No, I'm afraid not, my dear. I won't set foot in that house. You understand, don't you?"

"I do indeed," Mrs. Bartlett said kindly. There was no glint of mischief in her eyes now. Instead she seemed serious and thoughtful.

"Poor soul," she said, after Mrs. Hough had left them to return up Sixth Avenue. "I feel kind of badly that I used to speak so harshly of her. But then, I didn't know . . . and she certainly wasn't an ideal landlady . . . though no wonder she became somewhat peculiar and selfish."

"Jessica, stop talking in riddles," Mr. Bartlett grumbled, taking her arm while they crossed King Street. "David is furious that you deprived him of the story, so give, will you."

"It's the most fantastic thing again," Mrs. Bartlett began. David quickly slipped back of her to her other side so he wouldn't miss a word.

"You'll never guess who she is," Mrs. Bartlett went on. "Hold on to your hats. . . ." she warned. Then, very slowly, for much emphasis, she said, "Mrs. Hough is William Mac-Laughlin's granddaughter!"

"You're kidding!" David exclaimed.

"I can't believe it." Mr. Bartlett shook his head vigorously. "After all, this city has about eight million inhabitants, and there is such a thing as the law of averages."

"I tell you, she is," Mrs. Bartlett said, raising her voice. "If you had heard her tell the story directly, as I did, you wouldn't have doubted it for a second. Anyway, why doubt it? Nobody could make that one up, and why should she?"

For a couple of minutes they walked along silently. Somehow David sensed that he shouldn't press his mother to continue the story, and Mr. Bartlett didn't say anything either. When they reached their house they didn't go in, but lingered in front near the gate to the basement floor. It was a typical Sunday winter afternoon on Charlton Street, quiet and peaceful, not a soul around, but lamps burning brightly inside the old houses and the reddish sun lighting up the sky above the New Jersey shore.

Mrs. Bartlett looked up at their house, and when she turned her face toward Mr. Bartlett and David there was a puzzled expression on it. "Isn't it strange," she mused, "that to me this house means so much happiness and this same house meant nothing but misery to Evelyn Hough? When she was a young girl it threw a big shadow all around her." Mrs.

Bartlett seemed a little embarrassed at having used such flowery words. She pulled the collar of her coat up around her ears because the air was quite nippy. Then she walked over to their stoop, and in spite of the cold she sat down. Porto Rico, who had been visiting his latest fiancée across the street, spotted her, hurried over, and jumped into her lap.

"Let's go inside," Mr. Bartlett proposed.

"I'd like to sit out here for a minute. It's so nice," Mrs. Bartlett said. "I want to tell you what happened. You know, when Joseph died he left the house to William. Under the circumstances I find that most peculiar."

"I don't," Mr. Bartlett came back. "It seems quite logical to me that Joseph tried to make it up to William."

"But why should he, if he was innocent?" David asked.

"Even if he was, the gold disappeared in *his* house. That is to say, if there was any gold to begin with."

"You think there wasn't?" David asked.

"It's a possibility. As far as we can tell from the letters, Joseph never saw this sack of gold. It seems that William asked Joseph for a place to store his stake. Joseph showed him the drawer, and the next morning the gold was gone."

"Why didn't William show his stake to his brother?" David wondered.

"Both William and Joseph must have been strange men," Mrs. Bartlett said. "I don't know whether they always were, or only became that way after their experience in this house. Mrs. Hough told me that she remembers William as always cross and always carrying on about his lost stake and his thieving brother. What happened was that William went back to California—just as I thought. Remember, that last letter we have of his came from St. Louis. He was on his way back then. But he never made another stake. He ended up on a small dirt farm in Nevada with a wife and a son. The son was Mrs. Hough's father. The family came back east when she was a young girl and William an old man. Word had gotten through to Mrs. Hough's parents that Joseph had died and that William had inherited the house. Knowing how he felt, they didn't tell him, but they sold the little farm and brought him to New York. When William was told that he was Joseph's heir, he threw a fit and simply refused to accept the inheritance. Even though they were poor and lived here in furnished rooms, he wouldn't touch the property. Old as he was, he had it legalized in such a way that his son, as next in line, couldn't touch it either. He died soon afterwards, and that was the end of it. But Evelyn Hough told me that she and her family had a very hard time of it here. They couldn't make a go of it in the big city and they in turn became bitter about the lost inheritance. No wonder Evelyn Hough hates this house."

"Jeepers! What a mess," David said. He suddenly felt kind of angry at Mrs. Hough for telling his mother that depressing story.

"Let's go inside," Mr. Bartlett said abruptly. He too seemed disturbed. He lifted the cat to the street and helped his wife up the stoop. "I'll take you two to Luchow's for a fancy dinner. . . . Correction! You three!" he added, as he spotted Phoebe coming down the street with her small suitcase. "That'll cheer us up."

In the following week, the watch wasn't found, but Mr. Bartlett couldn't bring himself to question the girls in the studio. When, after some days, David somewhat timidly brought the subject up, his father told him that he had slept on it and had decided to hold off for a while. "It would be an awful strain on your mother," he concluded.

David understood that very well. Mrs. Bartlett had such a nice relationship with her workers. Again and again the sound of songs would come down to David—old ballads and folk tunes, which they harmonized in lovely, clear voices. At other times there was chatter and laughter. But always the thump-thump of the large loom, because in spite of the talking and the singing, the big wall hanging was proceeding slowly but surely. Already Mrs. Bartlett had accepted another commission—floor rugs for a suburban home this time.

The next Sunday after lunch David overheard a conversation between his parents about whether Mrs. Bartlett should let the three extra girls go, or retain them. "It's such a perfect team by now, and I certainly could use them all, but I can't get my mind off that watch, Carl," Mrs. Bartlett said. "It just couldn't disappear like that. It's too crazy, and something should be done about it for David. He has been so good about it."

David, who in a burst of generosity was cleaning the cage of Phoebe's parakeets, was wondering for a moment if he shouldn't declare his presence. Because it was an extraordinarily mild day he was doing his chore out in the yard near the back door and could hear every word that was said in the kitchen. Eavesdropping was strictly against the Bartlett code of decency. However, he decided to compromise with his conscience by whistling a tune. This didn't deter his parents from continuing with their discussion. Maybe they wanted him to hear what they were saying. "Were you absolutely sure about Charley's watch?" Mrs. Bartlett asked.

"How can you be sure of anything?" Mr. Bartlett countered. "The son-of-a-gun might have changed the band, for all I know. What did he say when the boys brought it back?"

"Some tiresome joke about how David had been a bad boy and hadn't deserved a watch. But Carl, we can't go around suspecting everybody. It's bad form, as they say in England. We'll end up as suspicious and strange as the MacLaughlins."

"What a horrible thought," Mr. Bartlett said. "I want to have another look at that drawer," he went on. "Right now."

At this point David decided to declare his presence, mainly because he wanted to be on the spot when his father examined the drawer. Carefully he placed his right hand under the cage and, after making sure he could balance it, let go with his left hand to reach for the doorknob. But leaning forward he touched the cage with his chest. There was a loud crash and the clatter of breaking glass. The birds screeched. David stood petrified. He heard his mother's voice saying, "Oh my goodness . . ." and then a window upstairs was opened and Phoebe's head appeared over the sill. "You stupid . . ." she screamed, "look what you did. . . . You've killed them. . . ." And then a loud wail, "Mother . . . Daddy!"

On the first floor, Grandma, who had come back with John the previous Sunday to "get away from it all" she said, and who had been taking her Sunday afternoon nap on the couch in the living room, opened the window and leaned out. She was still half asleep, but managed to call down, "Back to Boston!" and then shut her window.

Mr. and Mrs. Bartlett came hurrying to the yard. Squatting down, Mr. Bartlett examined the damage. "I think they survived," he said, and straightening up with the cage in his hands, he said to David, who was still unable to move, "Don't worry, feller. . . . They're alive."

Carefully he carried the cage inside and put it on the kitchen sink near the window. By now the birds were anxiously fluttering around. Then Phoebe burst into the kitchen. She was beside herself and sobbed as if her heart would break.

"Nothing serious happened," Mrs. Bartlett said soothingly. "David couldn't help it."

"He could . . . he could . . ." Phoebe sobbed. "I hate him, the big clumsy gorilla. . . ."

"Phoebe!" Mr. Bartlett said. "Now control yourself."
However, Phoebe wasn't even listening. "You poor darlings," she told the birds, and picking up the cage with a swoop, carried it out of the kitchen and ran up the stairs to her room.

"That won't do them any good," Mrs. Bartlett remarked. "I didn't even make sure that they didn't break a leg, or something." Mr. Bartlett made a move to go after Phoebe, but Mrs. Bartlett held him back. "Let me," she said. "First I've got to calm her down. Then you can examine them."

After she was gone, Mr. Bartlett turned to David, who was still standing near the back door trying to recover from the shock, and at the same time blaming himself for his carelessness. It had been stupid to balance the cage on one hand. He realized that. And when his father asked, "How in the world did it happen?" he answered, "I'm a jerk," and explained what he had been trying to do. "Well, it happened," Mr. Bartlett said. "Come on . . . let's go upstairs and inspect the damage."

They walked out of the kitchen and started to climb the stairs to the first floor, David behind his father. They could hear Phoebe's voice, still shrill with excitement, and the calming words from Mrs. Bartlett. On the first floor landing they realized that the sounds came from Mr. and Mrs. Bartlett's bedroom. "Here, now," Mrs. Bartlett was saying, "put some witch hazel on your face and stop blaming David. He didn't do it on purpose. It could have happened to anybody.

I'm sure the vet can put a splint on her leg. Just the littlest splint, darling, and she will be as good as new."

"I know she won't," Phoebe sobbed. "You just say that to make me feel better. Oh, I hate you all. . . ."

With that, they heard Phoebe's footsteps running across her parents' bedroom, making for the connecting door to her room. She closed it behind her with such force that the clap resounded through the whole house.

"She always . . ." David started, with the intention of saying that Phoebe didn't have to carry on that much, but he was interrupted by a bloodcurdling scream from Phoebe. An instant later something crashed to the floor in her room and Phoebe let out another terrible scream. Mr. Bartlett stopped on the landing in real alarm and then rushed up the stairs to the second floor landing. At the same time they heard Mrs. Bartlett running across her bedroom and John bounding down the steps from his study on the fourth floor. David ran after his father, but collided with Grandma, who had rushed out of the living room. "Lord save us," she cried, "the poor child."

Phoebe kept on screaming.

At the connecting door in her bedroom, Mrs. Bartlett pleaded, "Phoebe, please . . . what happened? Open up . . ." Apparently the connecting door was stuck. Phoebe started to sob.

The first one to reach Phoebe's door from the landing was John, but he couldn't get in. It was clear that Phoebe had locked the door when she had brought her birds to her room. Mrs. Bartlett, finding the door locked, had obviously gone through the connecting door and taken Phoebe back with her to her own bedroom to dab her face with witch hazel.

Mr. Bartlett, John, and David ran back to the master bedroom, where they joined Mrs. Bartlett at the connecting door. "I can't open it," she said in an agitated voice.

"I knew it, I knew it!" said Grandma, rushing into the room. "What's happening?" she then wanted to know, contradicting her first remark.

John gently pushed against the door, but something soft was blocking it.

"Ohh . . ." Phoebe wailed. Then they heard a slight noise back of the door, as if something was being dragged along the floor. Something else came clattering down. It sounded like a hail storm, and Phoebe screamed again.

John put his shoulder to the door, but the effort was wasted because now it opened so easily that John lost his balance and stumbled into Phoebe's room.

"Look out! . . ." Phoebe screamed.

CHAPTER ELEVEN

A Peaceful House

When Mr. and Mrs. Bartlett, David, and Grandma entered Phoebe's room, a most amazing sight met their eyes. First they saw the bird cage safely on Phoebe's desk, then they saw John leaning on Phoebe's vanity table, where he had landed after his tumble. An open box of dusting powder had fallen off and had left John's legs in a fine cloud of its contents.

Phoebe was lying on her stomach on the floor near the connecting door. They had to step over her, but this was easier said than done, because Phoebe was literally surrounded by the stones they had heard clattering down. These stones were of all shapes and sizes, and of an especially bright color. They were gold nuggets.

Right near Phoebe's leg was a long piece of board, the sight of which turned Mrs. Bartlett's face still a shade paler than it already was. On inspection this board proved to be a door lintel, with a pretty, carved-out flower decorating each end. The lintel had grazed Phoebe's left leg, and there was a small trickle of blood to prove it.

With a flick of her wrist, Grandma had a big, snow-white handkerchief out of her skirt pocket, and after pushing the gold nuggets aside with her foot as if they were dirt, she knelt beside Phoebe and dabbed the blood away. "It's nothing, my heart," she said. "Just a scratch."

At this, Phoebe, who had stopped sobbing, started to cry all over again. "I know, darling," Grandma said, "it's just too much all at once."

Mrs. Bartlett, taking a leaf from Grandma's book, brushed the nuggets out of her way and knelt next to Phoebe's head. However, she was so stunned by what had happened that she just sat there, her hands folded in her lap and staring at the space over the connecting door where the lintel had dropped out. Then she pulled herself together and started stroking Phoebe's hair.

The next one to recover the use of his vocal cords after Grandma was Mr. Bartlett. "Phoebe had better lie on her bed for a while. David, there's a small bottle of iodine in the medicine chest—you know where. Please bring it to me, and a glass of water." And when David made for the connecting door, he added, "Go around on the landing, will you? It's safer." With that he, too, looked at the space over the door where the lintel had been.

Only while David went on his errand did he realize that

his heart was thumping like mad. Somehow he knew that now all the mysteries of the house had been solved, but he was still too upset and confused to collect his thoughts. When he came back to Phoebe's room she was already lying on her bed, surrounded by all the members of the family. Grandma was perched near her head on the pillow, and Mrs. Bartlett at the lower end of the bed with Phoebe's feet in her lap. Phoebe had stopped crying and was wiping her face with Grandma's handkerchief.

Mrs. Bartlett put some iodine on Phoebe's leg, which made the victim groan. "That's what you get for slamming doors," Phoebe said with a wry smile. At this remark the whole family perked up, because it proved that Phoebe was on the mend.

"Don't regret it for a minute," said John. "You're the Queen of the Day." He was busily brushing the powder off his trouser legs with Phoebe's hairbrush, but he took time out to point to the objects on the floor.

"Are you out of your mind, using my hairbrush for that?" Phoebe asked him between gulps of water. Whereupon Grandma decided that Phoebe had fully recuperated, and got up from the bed.

"Is nobody going to clean up that stuff?" she asked, without the least bit of respect for the fortune in gold which was scattered over the floor. And to Porto Rico, who had finally found the courage to invade the battle zone, she said, "Get out of here, cat. We've got enough trouble without you."

"Oh jeepers, the birds . . ." Phoebe exclaimed, and bounded off the bed. She opened the cage and took the now quiet Parakeet-He and Parakeet-She into her hands. He seemed as right as rain, but She had a broken leg indeed.

Mr. Bartlett hurriedly made a little speech. "No more scenes, Phoebe. We'll take her to the vet in a little while. Put her back in the cage." And turning to John, "That's right, boy, take a good look." John had moved a chair to the connecting door and had stepped on the seat to get a close view of the space which had been behind the door lintel. He took something out of it and handed it to his father. "Careful, Dad," he warned, "you never know . . ." It was a pistol.

"Mercy me . . ." Grandma exclaimed, retreating to a corner, "this house is a grab bag of horrors. Put that gun down, Carl. . . . Stay back, children. . . ."

"What kind is it, Dad?" John asked from his perch.

"Cap and ball pistol," Mr. Bartlett reported, looking thoroughly pleased and not the least bit frightened. "The kind that would have been used by Abe Lincoln in the Black Hawk War. . . . Boy oh boy . . ." He added, "What else, John?"

This time John produced a small box, covered in dusty black velvet. He opened it himself. "Wow!" he started. "Look at that. . . ." He held the open box in his hand, describing a semicircle with it so everyone could see the contents. There were three glittering items, resting on the red satin lining. "Diamond pendant and matching earrings," he announced.

"Carl, put that gun down," Grandma commanded from the corner where she stood.

David and Mrs. Bartlett hadn't moved. David was standing next to John's chair and Mrs. Bartlett was sitting on Phoebe's bed. They were both still too stunned by the onslaught of events to budge.

Phoebe went up to John and took the velvet box from him. "Isn't it divine?" she squealed. "Can I take them out?"

Nobody answered or paid attention to her because John was removing another object, this time from the right corner of the space above the door. He handed it to David with a broad grin. It was the lost watch. Next he dug something else out of that same corner, which seemed to be hollow. That was the weaving sample which David had used as a bed for his watch.

"There you are," John said cheerfully, and added, "Dad, that drawer upstairs is really tricky."

"I know," Mr. Bartlett said. "It must have a trap which connects with a chute to that space up there over the door. And take a look at this. . . ." He picked up the door lintel and, upending it, showed John a small but sturdy hinge, still with a screw in it, on the right side. Immediately John groped with his right hand around the right upper corner of the door. He felt for something, pulled hard, and showed his father another hinge exactly like the first one. "There you have it," he nodded, "this was where the crook who lived here before the MacLaughlins hid the stolen goods. This was his vault. The lintel was a kind of door that could swing out on these hinges."

David still hadn't moved from the spot. He was watching the proceedings, which seemed to be happening at a distance. He felt completely stupefied. The watch was back on his wrist, and he had stuffed the weaving sample into his back pocket. In his right fist he clutched a couple of gold nuggets, and in his left hand he held a linen sack, which time had worn thin and which, in addition, showed a large tear. It was weighed down by about a dozen nuggets, still nestled in a bottom corner. He must have put the watch on, stuffed the weaving sample into his pocket, picked up the nuggets and the sack from the floor—but he had no recollection of having done any of it.

Mrs. Bartlett's voice made him turn around to face her. "David dear," she said, "come and sit with me here on the bed." Like an automaton David moved his legs and sat down. Mrs. Bartlett put a hand on his shoulder. "Take a deep breath," Mrs. Bartlett said. "That's what I'm doing. It helps." When David saw her smiling face, the tight feeling in his head went away. Mrs. Bartlett rubbed his cheeks with her fists. "There," she said, "you're getting some color again."

Grandma planted herself in front of them. She had her fingers closed around Parakeet-She. "Jessica, I suppose your veterinarian lives in the neighborhood," she said. "Give me his address. I want to get out of here, and I might as well take care of that poor bird before she breaks her other leg. I trust that by the time I get back, Carl will have put that pistol away—though I suppose that would be too much to expect —after which I will consult my timetable and go back where I came from, and where I should have stayed in the first place." Then, unexpectedly, she planted a kiss on Mrs. Bartlett's cheek and said, "Jessica, I'm so delighted for you. Isn't it thrilling?"

When Mr. Bartlett had made sure that the vet would receive a patient at this unusual time, Grandma left with her charge. Then Mr. Bartlett said, "Come on, people, let's get cracking. You kids, pick up the nuggets and put them in Phoebe's wastebasket. Here it is." He set the dainty silk container on the bed and John, Phoebe and David started scrambling for the nuggets, quite a number of which had scattered to the four corners of the room. When the last one had been retrieved, the wastebasket was half full. Mr. Bartlett, taking a stab at its value, judged them to be worth at least ten thousand dollars.

"Now we're rich!" Phoebe cheered, her eyes shining.

Mr. Bartlett shook his head at her. "Take it easy, Phoebe. I can't stand that kind of talk."

"I'm going upstairs to take another look at that drawer," John said, moving to the door. "Who's coming?"

But Mr. Bartlett detained him. "Just a minute. Phoebe, give me your big Webster dictionary. And where is your hockey stick?"

Phoebe produced both and they trooped upstairs to the boys' room. First Mr. Bartlett opened the secret drawer, and kneeling down, he shoved the hockey stick all the way in. Carefully, he turned the handle around in his hand till he was sure that the face of the curved end was resting downward. Then he pressed down. There was a soft, clicking sound. "Now shove the dictionary way back in," he told Phoebe, handing her the hockey stick. Phoebe complied, and they heard the book tumble down on the second floor.

"What I don't understand," David said, " is how my watch went down. I mean, it was much too light to spring the trap, and anyway, I put it in the front of the drawer. How could it slide so far back?"

"Good question," Mr. Bartlett nodded. "I've had the same thing on my mind. I think what happened was that the constant slamming of Phoebe's doors over a period of time upset the mechanism. Maybe the trap couldn't close all the way any more, and flat objects like the watch and the weaving sample could slip through. Friday morning a week ago, Sarah dusted the drawer. I asked her, and she remembered that she did. She must have closed it with too much force and made the watch slide back on the sample. I can't think of any other explanation."

"I bet anything can spring the trap now," John added. "David, let me have your baseball."

And sure enough, when John rolled the baseball in, again there was the soft click of the trap opening. "You don't hear a click for the trap closing," John remarked. "But let's go down and see if the ball got through."

"Of course it got through," Mr. Bartlett said while they descended the stairs to Phoebe's room. "Otherwise it would have rolled back, John."

They found the ball on the rug in front of Phoebe's bed. The dictionary was on the floor right under the connecting door.

"Some smart operator that crook was," John commented. "He must have had the whole works built in along with the house. And he must have paid a pretty price to the builder to keep him quiet."

"What crook?" Phoebe asked, momentarily confused. "You mean Joseph?"

"Phoebe . . ." David shouted impatiently, "he means Corcoran, the receiver of stolen goods who lived here first. He was the one who had the trap built, you dope. The Mac-Laughlins never knew about it as long as they lived. That's what was the trouble. Boy, are you ever stupid."

"Excuse me for living," Phoebe said haughtily, touching the diamond earrings she was wearing.

Mrs. Bartlett hadn't said a word while all this was going on. She had traipsed along on the different expeditions, but she had been unusually silent. Now she sat down on Phoebe's bed again and stared at the gold nuggets inside the wastebasket. Then she looked at the family.

"To think that it is irreparable," she mused, "and all that anger and frustration, the hatred and heartache, was actually for nothing. If those two people, those two brothers, had really trusted each other, nothing could have come between them."

They were all listening to her, their faces as serious as hers.

"There was never any real affection between those two—there couldn't have been," she went on, "certainly not from William's side. The minute the gold was missing he suspected his brother."

"If there is that much suspicion, there must be a reason," Mr. Bartlett cut in. "Of course, this is all conjecture on my part, but I have a hunch that William didn't get much help from Joseph before he went West. The fact that he went at all proves that he wasn't making out so well in the East. Well, Joseph was. He was able to buy a house. These buildings weren't cheap then, you know. In the 1870's this was one of the best streets."

"You know, Carl," Mrs. Bartlett said, "the whole thing makes me sad. All those lives that were ruined because of this. Think of Evelyn Hough and her childhood."

"Of course it's sad," Mr. Bartlett said. "But as a lawyer I can tell you that Evelyn Hough will be compensated somewhat. She is still the legal heiress of William. I'm pretty sure that these nuggets belong to her."

Phoebe gasped. "You're not going to give all that gold to Mrs. Hough, are you?" she asked. Then she clapped her hand to her mouth. "Oh, I hate myself," she said.

"What's the use of that?" came Grandma's voice. They didn't know she was back. But there she was, again all out of breath after climbing the stairs, and with Parakeet-She tucked neatly into a small box. "Where's the pistol?" Grandma wanted to know next.

"The pistol . . ." Mr. Bartlett echoed absent-mindedly. "Where is it? I forgot all about it. Oh . . . here it is." He took it from Phoebe's vanity table, where he must have set it down before.

"Carl Bartlett," Grandma said solemnly, "if you don't put that pistol safely behind lock and key, you will have seen the last of me. That rhymes," she added, much surprised.

"Don't worry, dear," John said kindly. "I examined that gun. It isn't loaded."

"You examined it!" Grandma thundered with terrible indignation. "And what did your parents say to that?"

"They didn't see me do it," said John.

Grandma shrugged her shoulders, admitting defeat. "Here is the bird," she said, lifting Parakeet-She out of the box. "She looks appalling with that bandage. You can take the splint off in ten days."

"Oh, my darling . . ." Phoebe cooed. Carefully she took the bird from Grandma's hands. "But she looks cute, Grandma. Look at her, everybody." She held Parakeet-She up for all to see. The bird didn't seem the worse for wear. Somehow she didn't even seem aware of the splint and the bandage on her leg.

"I think you should restore her to her husband," Mr. Bartlett suggested.

"You'd better watch them," Grandma said. "You never know with birds. They're a funny lot. Parakeet-He might attack her now."

"He wouldn't, either," Phoebe protested. But after she put Parakeet-She in with Parakeet-He she didn't move away from the cage.

Mr. Bartlett picked up the wastebasket. "I'd better put this away in a safe place. We don't want any more mysterious disappearances," he quipped. "Tomorrow in the office I'll make sure about legal ownership. Then you can call Evelyn Hough," he told his wife before leaving the room with the nuggets.

"I can't wait," Mrs. Bartlett said dreamily. "She'll be so delighted. Not only about the value of it, but also because now she will know that her family was honest at least—that it was all just a crazy coincidence."

"Gee," David said, "I wish I didn't have to go to school tomorrow. Mom, would you wait to call Mrs. Hough until I'm home? I want to hear what she says."

"Me, too," Phoebe said.

"Sure thing," Mrs. Bartlett promised them. She stretched herself. "Gosh, I'm kind of exhausted from it all. Let's have a nice, relaxing evening. How about playing some music, Ma?"

"I'll play all the music you want," Grandma said, "but before that you'll have to give me a cracker or something to sustain me. It's seven o'clock."

"Oh, how awful!" Mrs. Bartlett exclaimed, jumping up. "I forgot all about food. Everybody must be famished."

That night in bed, David was reviewing the whole history of the house. In his mind's eye he saw the row of brick houses built on the land full of trees and flowers, where Richmond Hill had been. The crook, Mr. Corcoran, probably some mean little runt, looking respectable in a fancy suit, high stiff collar, and stovepipe hat, was in a huddle with the builder. The builder was nodding his head, and then a small bag of money was given to him and they shook hands on the deal. Then David imagined all kinds of sinister-looking men going in and out of the new house. Or better still, Mr. Corcoran meeting with the thieves at the docks at Fulton Street, or in one of those old taverns along Canal Street, or maybe he would travel in the stagecoach to meet them somewhere in the country.

He pictured the police—in those early days they didn't even wear uniforms—searching the building. Mr. Corcoran would be sitting in the front parlor, calmly smoking a cheroot and grinning because he felt so safe about his secret vault. And then he died, and the house was turned inside out as they were still looking for evidence.

Then David pretended that he was living across the street, in the house where his grandfather had lived as a boy. Through the window he would watch Joseph and Catherine MacLaughlin looking over the building at 33½, never sus-

pecting the trap inside. Then he would see the cart, pulled
by horses, bringing the MacLaughlins' belongings, and shortly
after that the arrival of William, wearing a ten-gallon hat and

carrying his heavy luggage with his linen sack of gold. And
the next morning, William running out of the house and
Joseph calling after him.

John, who was used to gabbing with David at bedtime,
interrupted his fantasies. "What are you so quiet about?" he
asked.

"Oh, you know what I'm thinking about . . . the house,
of course . . . and all the things that happened in it."

"That'll keep you busy," John said. "I was thinking about all that money. I hope Mrs. Hough will share it with Mom and Dad . . . or give them part, at least. They deserve it."

"They sure do," David concurred.

"Good night, Boxhead," John said.

"Good night." David punched his pillow into its most comfortable shape and got ready for sleep. As usual, there was a little light in the room from the last glowing embers in the stove. It was quiet through the house. Peaceful, David thought. As if the house, with all its mysteries solved, was finally settling down around him.

DATE DUE

30 508 JOSTEN'S			